Praise for *ONE PER*

"*One Person Can't Make a Difference* is everything you could ever want from a pure, old school cyberpunk novel, but updated perfectly for our dark time. Ragolia's prose crackles and pops like electricity directly from the mainframe, a livewire for your senses running the taut narrative through every inch of your nervous system."

— Jordan A. Rothacker, author of *The Pit, and No Other Stories*

"*One Person Can't Make a Difference* confronts the traditional dystopian novel and shimmies its way beyond into new territory. Ragolia depicts familiar current conflict with secret hidden tracks and B-sides a reader would never expect in a cyberpunk novel. With a deep dive into darkness and storytelling of one character's spirit, Ragolia has created a world riddled with struggle and hope, light and dark, and within this balance, a reason to champion the underdog.

— Hillary Leftwich, author of *Ghosts Are Just Strangers Who Know How to Knock* and *Aura*

"Through the dystopian din, Ragolia pens a clarion call for radical hope and perseverance. *One Person Can't Make a Difference* plants seeds in the cyperpunk genre, bioengineers them with reverence and emotional precision, and cultivates a nourishing garden for the weary-hearted."

— O'Brian Gunn, author of *Furies: Thus Spoke*

"Nate Ragolia's *One Person Can't Make a Difference* is a slangy, manic blend of cyberpunk action and social commentary that will leave you ripping headlong through the streets of a future America in which the physical, moral, and intellectual trappings of humanity have melted away in the pursuit of unbridled capitalism and the technology it seems to deform at every turn. While Ragolia may ask the titular question of whether the individual can stand against the massed power of state, ethos, and, in truth, the species itself, he weaves in smaller, subtler concerns about what it means to be human and whether the loss of some elements of that 'humanity' might actually be for the best. Buy this book now!"

— Kurt Baumeister, author of *Pax Americana*

"Nate Ragolia does an amazing job both pulling us into his world and providing an escape-worthy narrative and mirroring our late-stage capitalist experience with the bleak future implied by literally selling one's body parts to make ends meet. Riveting, action-packed, and full of a message we need to hear in 2022."

— Addison Herron-Wheeler, editor at Q Publishing House, and author of *Respirator*

"With a touch of noire, our hopeful hero, Mr. Run Ono-Marks reads like a synth Humphrey Bogart, narrating his life and walking the rain-soaked pavement in the dead of night. Only our world in Ragolia's cyberpunk novel is long gone from Humphrey's. (Or is it?) Sci-fi is alive and well in this story, yet while laced in futuristic excitements like holos (holograms), "flying" "cars," and people made of robotic parts, we learn that when it comes to democracy and plain old right and wrong, not a damn thing has changed. This new world is mechanical and gross and controlling -- and high on the haves vs the have nots. With shortened, abbreviated words that make you feel like a robot yourself, there is a mechanical grind to the pacing. Yet, with a brevity of words, it is also quick to the punch which keeps you plugged into the story like a synth getting a recharge."

— Peppur Chambers, author of *Harlem's Awakening*

"*One Person Can't Make a Difference* is a well-written, fast-paced thrill ride! Author Nate Ragolia transports us to another time and place through the eyes of our "hero" Run Ono-Marks, who has his work cut out for him navigating this futuristic world, trying to figure out the "good guys" from the "bad" and which side he is ultimately on. This book will keep you guessing and entertained till the very end!"

— Nick Shelton, Author of *An Introvert's Guide To World Domination*

"*One Person Can't Make a Difference* is true cyberpunk, through and through. Deeply political and subversive, the novel is a strong yet hopeful indictment of the rampant corruption, inequality, and the lack of humanity in our world today."

— Johnny Redway, author of *The Cost of Living*

one person can't make a difference

A CYBERPUNK NOVEL

nate ragolia

SPACEBOY BOOKS

Denver, Colorado

Published in the United States by:

Spaceboy Books LLC
1627 Vine Street
Denver, CO 80206

www.readspaceboy.com

Text copyright ©2022 Nate Ragolia
Artwork copyright ©2022 Spaceboy Books LLC

Cover art features Free to Use photos by Mikhail Nilov
(https://www.pexels.com/@mikhail-nilov/)

First printed September 2022

ISBN-13: 978-1-951393-15-1

To the brighter future we can still build for ourselves.

one

"Cutting it a little close this week," Akari says as she engages the automated safety restraints around my ankles, wrists, and chest.

"Got tied up," I reply.

The haptic feedback from the pressure on my limbs and torso sends a shiver down what's left of my spine. They say you get used to it, but you really never do.

"You've got about twelve minutes left on here," Akari reads from the screen to her left that's wired into the port between my shoulder blades. "Surprised you didn't have a limp when you came in."

"Maybe I was trying to impress," I say.

Akari laughs politely. "Ready?"

"Am I ever?"

Akari chuckles.

"You're funny for a synth, you know..."

I don't have a chance to ask what she means by it because the Light crashes in like a waterfall. As my vision returns, I know right away that I'm Lucid. It's my apartment. The old one near the water. I hate this part. The screen chimes. I answer it. It's the Tseng County coroner. They're both dead. Twenty others too. Signal malfunction. They assure me that they didn't suffer. The County will name the intersection after them. Another crash of Light. The current apartment, back when there was stuff in it. Another screen call. The building manager. "You're four months behind, Ono! I'm tired of being generous." "It's Ono-Marks. They both gave me their na—" "I don't give two fucks about your parents unless they're paying me my money." Another crash. I'm on the old bike, the Kamaguchi SPS. My music suddenly cuts and a Holo pops into the HUD. "I'm not tipping you! Those burgers are already cold. Just throw them out." "Can't. Gotta bring them to your door. GPS." "Fuck you." "Fuck traffic, you mean." "What did you s—"

There's a surge. I feel like I'm going to piss myself and everything goes technicolor. Then more Light. "This procedure is irreversible, Mr. Ono-Marks. While your waiver seems to be in order, I am obligated by the Cap to ensure four-part authentication." I nod. "Please confirm your consent for the removal and replacement of the limb and organs indicated on the screen." I touch the green button. "Now confirm the rate of compensation and total amount of transfer." I touch the green button. "Good. Now just confirm these two waivers. The first waives our responsibility should you not survive the refit. The second waives your rights to reclaim sold components should you change your mind." I touch the green buttons. Another surge shakes me out of it briefly. Akari looks like an angel. More Light. In a cabin now, cramped. Hooked into the screen, making invitations for some Overcity soiree. * UNDER THE STARS * AN UNFORGETTABLE EVENING OF LIVE MUSIC, FOOD, AND LOVE * SCAN THIS INVITATION WITH YOUR RESIDENCY NUMBER AT ENTRY * PLUS ONES WITH PRIOR REGISTRATION ONLY * SECURITY ON SITE NO CRASHERS! * C U * XOXO MISS TASHA HARICOT. A message pops up as I set the text to submit: 'I know that I said *your choice* for the font and color, but I've been researching and I want something like this.' A similar invitation slides on screen. 'But, since this is what Mathilda Rains just used I want you to make something like it but better.' Fuck. 'The original scope didn't cover th—' 'If it's a problem, I'll hire someone else. There are literally tens of thousands of you.' The final surge. More like a wave. I feel warm all over. Mostly. I start blinking. Fast. Then the last Light. "Mr. Ono-Marks, this is the last available procedure." "Just show me the waivers and cut me the check." "This isn't a sustainable form of income." I laugh. Everything goes white. Then black. A pinch between my shoulder blades. I blink and open my eyes. Akari is there. Still angelic.

"Okay, Run. One hundred percent for another week," she says. "Don't waste it."

The restraints retract and the table slowly pitches vertical until my feet touch the end cap.

"Don't plan on it," I say. "Hopefully I'll make enough quick enough this week to be back before I'm under ten."

I step off the slab. Everything feels responsive again: arms, legs, hands, feet. Even my heart's whirring at maxcap. Nothing quite like a fresh charge. Nothing like the opposite either. Death.

"I figure you'd make good money fast, as synth as you are," Akari says, tapping at her screen to finalize my service. "Can't be that many folks who'd give it all up for parts."

"I think we'd both be surprised. You've seen how it is out there. Cash is tight."

"I don't recharge anybody like you, Run. Sure, an arm here or there. Livers in the barflies."

"Are you saying I'm special?" I ask.

"Aren't we all? Just ask the Bouquet."

"One big, happy family, embracing our differences, living in squalor, hand-to-mouth, empowered. And all getting what we deserve, yeah?"

She nods. "I was with you until the Cap stuff at the end."

"I'm a man without a country," I say, lighting a smoke.

"And a man without a body," Akari jokes.

If I hadn't seen her every week for eight years, I'd have taken offense.

"Now who's funny?" I say.

Akari grins.

I run a quick diagnostic on every part of me that isn't meat. All checks. Like always, brain, eyes, ears, nose are all that's soft. All that could fail me, regardless of a charge. I flick my left hand, all the attachments respond: lockpick, hackmod, print-mimic. I wave my right hand over my thigh. The casing pops, slides open, holster exposed. Iron jumps into my hand. I spin it, Western-style. Holster it. Close the casing. Toe blades extend and retract with a satisfying *shhhkk.* Feeling operational is the closest thing to feeling these days.

"What do I owe you?" I ask Akari.

"Don't worry about it. Loyalty bonus," she replies.

"Never heard of that in the Undercity," I say. "Loyalty's a symptom of blindness."

"Isn't everything?"

I tip my smoke to her and slide into my jacket. Two taps on the left sleeve and I issue Akari a gratuity.

"Fifteen? Someone's feeling generous," she says.

"Loyalty bonus."

She offers an exaggerated wink and starts about setting everything back to zero for the next synth on the day's schedule.

"It must be kinda depressing," I say, running mechanical fingers through my natural hair. I catch her cocking her head curiously, distorted, blurry behind my reflection in the sterile chrome cabinet doors.

"Recharging folks day after day," I continue. "Knowing it'll never be enough."

Akari reboots the charging station. The lights in the room flicker. A warm hum fills the air.

"Everybody dies, Run. I get to give them another week, and they'll do with it what they can," she says. "It's not noble or anything either. It's just what I have to do."

"Maintain the status quo."

She laughs.

"You're in a shitty mood. And no. It's not about maintaining the status quo. It's about maintaining synths who might have a chance to change it. Like you."

Now I laugh.

"Sure," I say. "If I keep picking up gigs every day, one of them is bound to be the one that changes the whole system. Just gotta weed through the rides, deliveries, ticky tacky short-term project bullshit first, yeah?"

Akari slides across the room, taps at her screen, turns on the newsfeed.

"You wouldn't keep coming here week after week to grab another 168 of life if you didn't see purpose in it," she says. "And I wouldn't keep coming here lighting synths up each week if I didn't."

"Maybe I'm just stuck in a rut."

She doesn't answer. She's lost in the screen. An ad for tonight's fight in the NeonCube ends with a typically bloodied face. Fades to another story about the Noncons. Out there in the Acid Wastes, starving in their makeshifts, tattered clothes and disease. Working together, collaborating, to all have enough, and still failing. Then a tragic lingering shot. Green mist rising off a young one, skin slowly evaporating. Then the Cap corporate military setting up razor wire, drawing lines in the sand, firing shots at Noncons with their own makeshift weapons. "Don't even dream of coming back, Noncon trash!" Bouquet corporate troops on the other side, kicking the lines away with their boots, jawing. "We'll always make room for you back in the Commonwealth when you're done *experimenting*." The Noncons keep going about their business, trying not to die out there. "Despite attempts by the Commonwealth to help, the Noncons continue to reject offers of support. Tragic stuff." The story transitions. "On a lighter note, tomorrow begins Recognition Day, when citizens of the Overcity choose one lucky Undercity citizen to enjoy the first night of

The Week of Revelry, commemorating the establishment of the Overcity, as if they lived Up Top. So someone is going to go to sleep pretty happy tomorrow night..."

"Sorry," Akari says. "What'd you say?"

"Nothing. See you next week."

As the charge clinic door slides open, Akari grabs my shoulder.

"Don't forget your parking card." She hands it to me. "It's validated."

"Thanks for saving me the second trip."

She smiles.

"Say, if you need any replacement parts—that left leg is looking a little rough—we can work something out. Just let me know."

I nod. "Will do."

Akari's clinic opens on its adjacent parking lot. The lot is nearly empty, with a couple sporty Rambler XKs, a few Transit Haulers. The rest are Denco PMs, cheap boxes with only three speeds and limited flight range. Standing out is my Kento M6. Six speeds. 300 klick flight range. Built in solar refuel. The only thing I managed to keep when they died.

It's just me and the wet echo of night. Lamps cast shadows on the pavement, illuminate the falling rain. It's quiet. Nothing to do in the Seventh other than pawn stolen shit, buy synth parts on the sly, or score pills. If you want something semi-upstanding to do on a night like this you're in the Fifth or the Second. Or you're in the Overcity, but no one who'd be down here's gonna go up there.

The Commonwealth is a megacity, 700 klicks square. Nothing but buildings, streets, alleys, and people, all fifty-million of us. There are nine sectors. I live in the Ninth, in a Resettlement tower of one thousand units, each one about thirty meters square. The Ninth is full of Resettlement towers, production facilities, and powerplants. The view when the cooling towers off-gas is supposedly like Aurora Borealis. Never seen the real thing.

Ten klicks above the nine sectors, held up by dozens of pillars and high-tension pulleys, is the Overcity, making everything below it the Undercity. The Overcity is covered with the Field, an energy dome that keeps the Wastes beyond the Commonwealth, and the acidic weather, from mixing with the Overcity atmosphere. The Field also filters the sunlight and brightens the stars at night. There are parks, animals, beaches, mountains. Anything a life of leisure could need. The Overcity is for the fortunate people. The corporate bosses visit the Undercity once a year to keep up appearances. Employee outreach. Otherwise, down here doesn't exist beyond a cautionary tale. "There but for the grace of Cap..." and all that. The Cap's offices are in the Overcity. The Bouquet's too. Puts direct meaning to top-down governance. Especially when Undercity folks votes count for half... "to balance the population disparity and ensure a sense of fairness."

The Cap runs things at the moment. Their angle is rugged individualism. If you're in the Overcity you earned it, if you're not you earned it too. You get what you deserve, and for most folks that means less than nothing. They spend cash on the corporate militaries —whichever bids lowest that day—to "quell rampant violence in the Undercity," and on improving the Overcity. Cap officials are all corporate bosses, current and former, and they work for themselves, save for the illusion of care they show their Overcity constituents. The Bouquet reliably opposes the Cap. They talk about diversity, equality, and progress. They call out the Cap for every police riot and extrajudicial execution. They promote understanding and collaboration to make the Commonwealth work for everybody. Even pushed for a compromise making Undercity folks votes worth three-quarters. Didn't pass. The Bouquet didn't have the seats. They rarely do for things like that. It was close though. Close enough that the Bouqs upheld their part of the deal and gave the Caps their cuts to Undercity healthcare and housing maintenance.

The Commonwealth is simple. Watch your back. That's it. Someone wants to pick you out or off, they will. Doesn't matter if you're Over or Under. It's why I only take gigs posted on the Board. Vetting. You can't trust folks much more, but OppTech's customer service is better armed and trained than any corporate militia. 100% satisfaction guaranteed. The gigs don't pay great, never have. But they beat being a full-timer. Eleven months on, two weeks off, two weeks of instruction and re-education. Eat, piss, smoke, and shit at your desk for max efficiency. Four hours for rest with Hypersleep tech for enhanced alertness and reduced suicidal thought. Not for me. I'd rather run down to zero and die in my Kento than live like that.

I've done my share of freelance up there and down here. Started with the easy stuff after my parents died. The front pages gigs. Mostly rides, above board deliveries, small programming projects, design work. Reputable. I did upwards of thirty a day, working all hours, exhausted, hungry, sad. Debt still piled faster than those gigs paid. Got desperate. That's when I started going synth. Supplemental income, but even that wasn't enough. So I went full synth. Still had to sell everything I had left, empty the apartment of any fragments of before. Also when I started digging deep in the Boards. Way down to the better paying stuff, the gigs in margins. Not quite legal. Not quite not. Just peripheral. Those gigs are more dangerous, but they pay better. Not even that much better, but at least they're worthwhile.

Gigs are a great equalizer. I don't give a damn who you are when I take a gig, just what the gig is. Overcity bigwig needs extra bussers at a wedding, they need me. Undercity kid wants pizzas delivered for a birthday, they need me. Hacking. Deliveries. Light security. Lock "smithing." I'm the synth for you. And it's nice to be needed. And I do quality work whenever possible. It gets done, however it gets done. And no one's ever asked. Not that they'd want to know.

Really, no one with cash wants to know the person they're giving it to. It's easier that way. Distance keeps you clean. When you're buying you're buying. When you're bought you're bought.

I activate the retractable hood on my jacket. Couldn't catch a cold if I wanted, no lungs to infect, plenty of nanos to obliterate anything that doesn't belong. Just still don't like my hair getting wet. Too distracting when there are better things to be distracted by.

Everything in the Commonwealth glows neon from the holos. In the Overcity, the light drowns out the stars above, rivals the clean sunlight coming down through the Field. Down here, all the flickering pink and blue and green dances on the evermoving moving plume of smog slowly working its way to the overwhelmed turbines that push it out into the Wastes. When I was a kid, there was a campaign to accelerate the turbines, move the smog faster. It never took because the Overcity folks didn't care for the wind it created up there.

Otherwise the Undercity is wet and black. Rains roll off the Wastes and slip beneath the Overcity where they settle on us for days or weeks, but it's never enough water to wash away the grime or push

14

down the smog. It's either grim or grimmer, a trickle of sun from above or a flood of rain, depending on the time of day. And always the colorful glow of the holos, and the chimes of the chronopanes.

Chronopanes were the only thing the Cap and Bouquet completely agreed on. Their last great bipartisan public works project was installing them everywhere. You'd always know when you were late for a gig, being surveilled, or whether a Quarterly was due in a day or a day ago.

Pretty though, this neon trash heap, with rain and light collecting in luminous puddles swirling with gasoline.

The gullwing of my Kento M6 swings open as I step in range. I lean down and wave the validated parking card at the boot clasping the left front tire and wheel. As it retracts into the surface of the lot, I settle into the driver's seat, tap the ignition, and boot up the Board.

"This is OppTech Worx. Welcome back Run Ono-Marks," the unthreatening monotone voice says. "Enter keywords for Commonwealth-wide gig search, or select Favor—"

My fingers are faster after a charge. Plus I hate listening to that voice. Listings scroll down the screen.

Nothing in my grade. All below. Doesn't mean the rent won't be due. Doesn't mean I won't owe quarterlies. Doesn't mean charges will become free. Doesn't mean what I owe on my parents' place'll be forgiven. I mark fifty opps, nothing I want, not really, and make my offers.

All of a sudden, feels like a hot blade against my neck. I can't help but wince and cry out.

"SURGE WARNING! POTENTIAL OVERCHARGE! SURGE WARNING! POTENTIAL OVERCHARGE!"◙

Goddamn Akari using hacked equipment. No wonder I felt so good. My fault for going there. Can't beat the price. I collect myself, run another diagnostic. All checks.

The Board chimes. "Your personalized OppTech Worx matches are avai—"

Nothing. Not one fucking gig. Same old feedback bullshit. Too expensive. Not enough experience. To get some organs from the heli to the hospital? Previous bad experience. That fucking statue was missing its arms when I picked it up. Nothing. I'll have to try again in an hour. Fucking OppTech Worx algorithm's been fucking me since the update two months ago, keeps feeding me garbage matches. Doesn't help that buyers think this is supposed to be white glove, expect miracles with a smile and a tip of a hat.

I close OppTech Worx and check the Commsite. Nothing but ads. The Cap needs cash to keep the Bouquet from leading a coup. The Bouquet needs cash to resist the tyranny of the Cap. Fund a surgery. Fund a treatment. Fund a project. Fund a traveling art exhibition. Fund the Overcity Preservation Society. Fund Undercity Dwellers for Clean Air. The monthly bill for Ono-Marks Resettlement Fees. I wonder how bad it's gotten.

"Dear Run Ono-Marks, o

Your Resettlement premium is overdue. Late fees of C3,750 will be applied if minimum payment of C1,250 is not met by 06/10/93. If necessary, acquire a hardship waiver by saying 'waiver.' Thank you for using Commonwealth Resettlement Services." o

Seven days. Not that it matters. I'll be paying the Resettlement until I can't take another charge. Funny, to lose your parents, and be stuck with their debts. Funnier, to have those debts mean your home in the Overcity is now property of the Commonwealth. Funniest, they'll move you to the Undercity into a smaller, older place, for price. They took the house, everything we had, marked it down by 70%, sent me a bill. C1,250 every month on top of rent, food then, charges now, fuel, anything else that'd make me feel actually alive. Don't like it? Can't do it? Pay it three times for being late. How's that for resettled? It's why I sold everything. Arms first. Then legs. Then heart, lungs, stomach, liver. Et cetera. Et viscera. Paid down the interest that way. Chipped the balance down to C11,440,210. The Commonwealth generously offered me a payment plan. Would've been lower if I opted for Corporate. Couldn't do it. Freelancing at least meant pretending I was outside of it all. Right after they died, I needed to pretend. Now, I'm just used to it. It's comforting being an objective synth in a senseless society.

"Looks like you could use a spot of luck there?" some shadowy fuck says, sidling toward the Kento.

My thigh compartment pops, iron jumps into my hand. I aim and glare.

"Who asked you?"

The character, trenchcoated and masked holds up his hands.

"Whoa now. I saw you come out of that clinic," he says. "Happened to overhear your Resettlement troubles too." He points to his ears, they twist, click and slide out on arms away from his head. Synth tech.

I keep my gun on him. "I don't need your help. I suggest you hit the skids."

This trenchcoated, shadowy synth chuckles.

"Are you quite certain of that? What if I could offer you solutions to your problems in exchange for a single gig?"

I lower the pistol. Aim for the knees now.

"That sounds like bullshit to me," I say. "No gig's like that. Not here or anywhere."

"This is a unique opportunity," he says, reaching toward an interior pocket of his trenchcoat. "If you'll permit me?"

I nod, raising my aim just in case.

The shadowy synth produces a miniholo and holds it out, palm up. An official looking woman, suited, seated behind a big, important desk looks straight ahead, starts talking.

"We need someone special, someone who has sacrificed everything... well, almost everything. They will help us finally stop the abuses of the Cap. All we ask is for a meeting with the proper candidate. In return, we offer C15,000,000 and PerpetMot upgrades for any synth components they have or wish to add.

This is a chance to make a difference and make a lot of cash."

The miniholo cuts out, disappears into the shadowy character's hand.

"So?" he asks. "What do you think? All that cash and synth parts that will never need a charge again."

"PerpetMot and C15,000,000? That's too good to be true."

"I assure you, it's true and only a tiny fragment of their coffers."

I lower my iron. What do I have to lose?

"Good. You're considering it," the shadowy character says. "Take this. It's geotagged for the meeting point. Go there tomorrow. 7pm. Come alone. They will take a meeting to assess if you're a fit."

"Seems like I'm already a fit if you followed me here," I say.

The shadowy character chuckles again. "Look at you, synth from the neck down. You *have* given up almost everything, haven't you?"

"Preying on the desperate can be treacherous work," I say, drawing the hammer back with my thumb.

Another chuckle. "Yes. Of course. Well, I suppose I'll see you tomorrow or I won't. The choice is yours. There are always other candidates."

I lower the weapon, reholster it. Thigh compartment closes. I look at the miniholo, it opens again, the message restarts. I look up. The shadowy character is gone.

Tomorrow. 7pm. Worst case: they try to kill me.

two

Driving is the best part of my days. The Kento M6 slashes the tight corners, slips through the alleyways. Programmed in all the best routes by times of day. Shortest and fastest. The graviscopic suspension keeps the ride smooth, even when slamming from sixth to first and kicking in the vertical thrusters to go over that which can't be gone through. Don't like sitting in traffic. Don't have time for it.

Traffic everywhere. Screen says it'll take forty-five minutes to get from my apartment in the Ninth over to the Loop. Should be twenty. Then I notice the problem. Hundreds of new vehicles flooding from the

Overcity. I can't believe I forgot. Recognition Day traffic's always shit. All those Overcitiers venturing down below to find their last-minute charity cases. Nothing like a train of the fanciest of the fancy rolling through your own personal hell to gawk at you like they're picking out lobsters from the tank. Be better if they just ate one of us each year. More definitive, poetic. I'm going around them. Don't need Recognition and definitely don't need to be held up by it. I slide the Kento up onto the sidewalk, speed up, wait for an opening and slide back through to the other side. Weave my way to the Loop. I can make up ten minutes easy. Snake around another beater, put the pedal to the floor. Third slides to fourth slides to fifth.

The screen lights up red and blue. Speakers start screaming. Goddamn. Must be a corporate escort with all these Overcitiers. I check the rearview. Sure enough. Two LyfTek patrol cars, projectors bathing me in red light. Shame before blame. One of the hired goons pops up on the dash screen, mustached like he saw it in a movie.

"Vehicle operator, you are participating in unsafe maneuvers. Halt your progress and pull carefully over for LyfTek Motorist Safety engagement."

I let off the pedal, pull the Kento to the side, flick it into neutral, turn off the engine. Lower the driver's side window, lay my hands on the steering wheel, wait patiently, quietly, still. Absolutely still. You don't mess with these corporate cops. Leave the engine running, they'll magpulse it and you're going nowhere for hours. Forget to lower the window, they'll shatter it. Move a centimeter, they'll jab you with a shock baton or worse. Twitchy fuckers. Always reading from a script, waiting for something to go wrong. And when you're waiting for something often enough, it usually happens, real or imagined.

Couple years back, I'm taking the Kento to the shop and get held up because of the very same faulty signal I was heading to repair. That cop was from JoyLand Undercity Security. Chip on his shoulder the size of the Wastes. Sidles up, starts barking at me. I'm just waiting for him to wear himself out when he reaches in through the window and grabs the wheel like he's going to keep me from taking off or something. "I'm not going anywhere, *sir*." "Then get out of the vehicle. I've got a feeling about you. Synth in a car like this. What're you hiding, son?" "Nothing. Just driving to get my signal fixed. I'll show you." I reach for the lever and BAM! That JoyLand cop shoots me square in the chest. Being mostly synth has its advantages. The gunshot gets all these Undercitiers riled up. A group of them slide over, grab the JoyLand corporate cop and overwhelm him. I don't stay, but I hear a couple more gunshots and see a scrum in the rearview. If I thought I'd win, I'd have sued for the repair costs. C3,300 just to remove the bullet and reform that torso section. Of course, Akari is cheap, so who knows what the parts were really worth. About a week later, the newsfeed's abuzz with Overcitiers raising money to help the corporate cop recover from his injuries. Make him into a hero. And stories about the dangers of the Undercity run hot for a month until folks get tired of it.

I'm more careful now. Always follow procedure to a T. It's not worth the inconvenience to do anything else, as much as I'd like to. Besides, most of them are tragic little pukes looking for a chance to play hero and make cash at the same time. That greed component makes a difference. Most of the time you can offer them some cash and they suddenly forget they saw you doing anything wrong. These corporate cops all have overlapping jurisdictions anyway, usually something like "to protect and serve the customers of Company and the zones of the

Commonwealth in which they live, work and play."
And who the customers are never really changes. It
ain't Undercitiers, save for a single, big annual
purchase of something wanted, or a trickle of
necessities. Customer service, like morality and ethics,
are Overcity concerns. Down here, you stay invisible,
stay charged, and stay alive. These cops just keep
things the way they are. They're a symptom, not the
disease. And I'm no doctor.

The LyfTek Motorist Safety boy approaches the
window. He's pale and quavering.

"Mr. Ono-Marks, do you understand why I've
stopped you?"

I keep my hands on the wheel, eyes forward.

"I imagine I was driving a little recklessly," I say.

The corporate cop leans down.

"You were," he says. "And you'd be smart to
watch that in the future. But that's not why I pulled
you over."

I can feel his beady eyes crawling all over me.

"You're mostly synth, aren't you Mr. Ono-Marks?"

"Nothing illegal about it," I say.

"Not when the components are reputably
obtained. No," he says.

"You saying something?"

The LyfTek Motorist Safety officer holds up a screen. My picture's on it. There's a long list in red that's too small for me to read beside it.

"Pretty much all of these parts have been marked stolen, Mr. Ono-Marks. You know that's a crime, don't you?"

I keep staring straight ahead.

"If they were stolen, I was not made aware of that at the time of acquisition," I say.

"But you think it's possible they were stolen? Is that correct, Mr. Ono-Marks?" he asks.

I don't answer.

The cop flicks out his shock baton, air crackling around it.

"I'll ask again. Did you think that your synth parts could have been stolen, Mr. Ono-Marks?"

I still don't say a word.

He cracks the baton against the still exposed part of the driver's window. If I hadn't replaced the glass with shatterproof he'd have broken it.

"Don't make me ask again!"

I slowly turn my head, hands still on the steering wheel, torso still square in the seat.

"What do you want? One hundred? Two?" I ask. "You can't want much because you know that file says

27

there's zero evidence of theft and that all of the serial numbers on those parts were decommed and written off. Tell me the price and let me get on with my day."

The officer bites his lip. I can tell he's considering trotting out some noble lie about protecting innocents. He considers it for longer than necessary because he's probably just now extorting without his training wheels.

"Two hundred, you shitcan synth," he finally says. "Two hundred right now and I don't claim assault."

I sigh.

"Fine. I'm going to transfer two hundred to you now," I say. "I'll have to touch my band so I'm going to reach for my wrist. Okay?"

The twitchy LyfTek Motorist Safety cop nods unconvincingly.

"Okay. I'm going to reach for my wrist now. To transfer the two hundred."

I take my left hand off the wheel and reach to the inside of my right wrist. I tap at the synth flesh and a basic screen appears with the diagnostic menu, my ID, cash. I clock the cop's badge number from his uni and send the two hundred. A chime emits from his badge, confirming the transaction.

"There. You've got your two hundred," I say, teeth gritted.

"That's right, Mr. Ono-Marks," he says. "I've got it. That's for cooperating with LyfTek Motorist Safety. Have a pleasant evening."

At that, he turns back to his corporate-issue squad car, kills the lights and deactivates the alert on my screen.

I wait for him to pull away, watch the redshift of the tail lights, before turning the Kento back on. Two hundred was pretty cheap. The kid was new, inexperienced. A regular shakedown runs five hundred easy. Just happy he didn't mess with the car. Happier I didn't have to deal with him further, didn't have to kill him. That's a real good way to ruin the evening, and I've got places to be.

Once I finally hit the Loop, I slap the Kento into overdrive and have fun with it. A holo-projected neon blue, multi-tiered highway in three-dimensional space probably seemed like a good idea at the time, but in practice it's total shit. Gotta be a crack driver to get anywhere fast, dodging around folks waiting for their screen to tell them when to exit, when to turn. Every day there're ten deaths on the Lower Loop. It's better on the Upper Loop. Everything's better up top. Only

about ten deaths a year. But then, they have rack and lane markers, functioning sign holos, and AI speed control. Not that it mattered for my parents. The Kento's needle tickles 300 kmph. I'm in the zone. Haulers, Ramblers, Dencos, even some PineTek Travelers, blur into their own tail lights as they speed by. I catch a kid's face, pressed against the back window of a Denco PM. Gasps as the silver streak of Kento M6 rips past. Probably felt that shitty frame shake too. I'm passing under a Hauler, over a Traveler, and between two Ramblers when the miniholo chirps and illuminates. Next exit. I cut across the Lower Loop from interior to exterior, zigzagging down along the way, slap the stick into first, stomp the brake and disengage the vertical thrusters. The Kento breaks out of the aquamarine glow, peels off over a normal asphalt street and sets down smooth. Safe as houses.

I park the Kento two blocks from the meeting point on the miniholo. Better to not attract the attention that a limited edition '85 sportcoupe tends to. Never been to this part of the Fourth so caution is necessity. Thought it was all storage. From the looks of the windowless cement and last-gen waste bins, no one should be here. More of a place for sanitation mechs that citizens, even Undercitiers. Gotta be a

setup, and a lazy one. I set the security field on the Kento to max, grab and activate the miniholo, light a smoke, and climb out.

Take soft steps from the Kento around the adjacent building, following the miniholo like a compass. Nearly run into a sani-mech, huddled in the gutter, rooting at the storm drain pulling something meaty out. Little bot's struggling, claw clutching, its stubby jack-like legs pulsing up and down for leverage. Mech tumbles back, balance stand catches it, and triumphantly holds up the prize. Looks like an arm. Blasted all to shit, but that's definitely a hand at the end of it. Fingerprints charred black. A hit disposal. Now gone ass up. I wonder who's going to fry for it? Probably no one, unless they're completely disconnected from the Overcity.

One block out, I smell something. Smoke. Not fire smoke. Not smog. It's mixed with something noxious, cloying. My eyes start to water, so I flip up my hood and drop the mask and visor. HUD tells me it's CS, auto-calibrates the mask to filter it out. Something's up. I take a last look at the miniholo, deactivate and pocket it. Pop my thigh compartment, iron ready. Walk down the final block as the HUD assesses the situation. Closer I get, more CS in the air, and now barrel smoke, residue. Whatever it is, it's hot. I just don't know how it's so quiet. I stand, back to the wall, and activate my cloak. The field slips over me, mimicking the cement surface of the building with a wavering shimmer. I won't blend in for long, or at all if I move too fast, but it'll give me a couple seconds advantage.

Slide toward the meeting point, slowly, silently. That's when I get it. Blasts of light splash behind the glass of the adjacent warehouse. Silhouettes run by in obvious panic. I watch one stop, turn to look back, collapse in a heap. Smoke seeps out the edges of the windows, billows out where another silhouette tries propping the pane up, gets shot trying to climb through. Pandemonium. But without the noise. There's an aural disrupter out in front of the warehouse, little pyramidal box with three nodes extended, spinning a web of neon pink light that covers the warehouse in a dome. With that in place, no sound can get through. Everything else can, but smoke in the Undercity isn't something to be surprised about, CS gas isn't either. This is a coordinated hit.

Crouch down, lay out, and hug the street, still blending in because of the cloak. I crawl into the aural disrupter field and press myself up against the building. Peer carefully into the windows, get a taste of what's going on behind closed doors. Explosions rattle the exterior. Gunshots pop and ring. The screaming. "Please don't. We don't know where it came from. Please!" "You shouldn't have crossed the Cap." "We didn't do anything! Don't. Please. We'll do anything you want. Just let us live!" "Then why is there so much void sitting around ready to be packaged? You're selling this without the approval of the Commonwealth. And the penalty is death." "You've killed them all! We don't know anything. We just sleep here! Stop. Please!!" Pop. Pop. Pop. Executions. No more screams or protests. The gunmen look like PalCorp militia, purple bands on their helmets. The gunned are mostly kids, women. Drugrunners. Void isn't even serious or cash-heavy. Just two hours of feeling less like shit, tasting things a little more intensely, and seeing some colors. Probably fifty folks in my building sell it. Doesn't make a lot of sense that the Cap would want to hit this. Nor that they'd hire PalCorp to do it. Using a sledgehammer to hang a painting.

I hear the militiamen tromping back out of the building, talking to each other. One of them saunters over to the aural disrupter and switches it off, pockets it.

"I don't think they knew anything," one says to the others. "Might've just been a drug op."

The leader shakes his head. "Nah. The Cap wouldn't send us on bad intel. They're working with the Bouqs one way or another. Probably funneling cash. Don't be fooled by their acting, boys. These weren't good people. We did what we had to."

"They better pay us for this void," says another, carrying armfuls of the drug tablets. "I'm not leaving it here for some Undercity urchin to pick up and sell himself."

"Fine. Make sure you all take some for yourselves too," the Leader says. "Use it later or sell it. I'll log everything after."

The group of PalCorp militia mill around for a few. Not one of them notices me and I don't dare move. The leader takes off his helmet, clips it to his belt, pulls a prot-bar from his uni pocket and starts munching. Imagine being able to eat after killing a bunch of women and kids. If I still had a stomach, it'd be turning. The other PalCorp folks start rooting through the void, picking out their take, while chattering about mundane shit like Recognition Day,

34

evening plans, promotions, shit they jerk off to. Funny to call yourself a soldier when the only discipline you have is to kill on command, without a second thought. They'll sleep well though, probably get home upgrades as commendations. The newsfeed eats up stories about drugrunners and the Cap knows how to craft realities. No one in the Overcity will ever know who got killed or what they were doing. They'll just know they're a modicum safer in a Commonwealth besieged by evils. No one in the Undercity'll probably know either, but only because they won't have the luxury of time or the proclivity to find out.

I wait there, while the PalCorps jaw at each other and pat each other on the backs. The leader gets on a call with someone important. Sounds like the Cap checking in but no way to know without getting closer and I'm not moving. After he ends the call, the Leader counts off his crew. Does it again. Grabs one of the soldiers surrounding the cache of seized void.

"Where's Two-Three-Two?" the leader barks.

The soldier shrugs. "Thought he was already out."

"I don't see him. Do you see Two-Three-Two?" the leader raises his voice. "Who's seen Two-Three-Two?"

The other soldiers shrug similarly, shake their heads. Fine-tuned killing machines. Then another soldier, smaller than the others, emerges from the doorway. Marches crisply toward the leader, weapon aimed at the ceiling, stock in palm like something out of a History course.

"Two-Three-Two reporting," he says. "I've just completed a full sweep of the target. No signs of secret passageways or recently blocked access points. No signs of Bouq activity. And given the layout of the cots and personal effects, I'd venture this was some kind of orphanage. I did a scan on the void when we entered, and its atmospheric signature doesn't match this warehouse. It wasn't from here at all. Must've been planted. With your permission, sir, I think it would be prudent to notify the Cap of these discrep—"

The leader is quick on the draw. Easy when you're with friendlies. Fires a shot right between Two-Three-Two's visor and chest plate. Bullet rips through the neck, blood mist explodes. Two-Three-Two's head tips forward, jolts back, and rolls back, dangling from a sinew or two of muscle. Body drops like a rock and falls forward. Helmet bounces on the sidewalk, lands with a wet thud, rolls three-quarter turns. The other PalCorp soldiers stop their chatter for a moment, not long. The leader reholsters his weapon.

"Drag Two-Three-Two inside and light the place," he says. "I'll report the casualty to Pal and the Cap. Seems that Two-Three-Two got locked inside when the Bouqs went suicidal. Tragic. Looks like we're all getting Line Of Fire points this week."

The other militiamen dutifully drag the corpse inside. One gathers the head, rolls it in through the open door. As they exit again, they toss GelOrange canisters. Luckily, the timer is loud enough to dance to. I wait until they clear out, marching away down the block. I hear a Hauler rev up, probably one of those retrofits for crowd control. Some neothrash song starts playing. One of them lets out a hoot and holler and the Hauler peels out.

I deactivate my cloak, stand slowly. The canister's countdown meanders to its end. I see it flashing among the corpses of women and children. I could probably get in and switch it off but who'd I tell. It wouldn't do any good. It'd never make the newsfeed. Besides, it's probably better to die anonymous here. No costs passed on to next of kin. No burial debt. No tarnished names. They just disappear.

I drop my mask and visor, retract the hood, and light a smoke. I take out the miniholo and light it up. This was the meeting place. Why would that shadowy figure want me to meet him at an orphanage anyway? Was it a setup? Who would set me up? I'm nobody. It didn't make sense. I'd have to figure it out, but not tonight. I need a drink. Maybe some void of my own. Seen too much. I turn and start back toward the Kento when a rock hits me square in the back. I grab my pistol, whip around and aim.

The shadowy figure, huddled between two trash processors, in the adjacent alley.

"Please, follow me Mr. Ono-Marks," he says. "You've done very well. You're clearly smart enough not to get caught."

I keep my aim. "This was a test?"

"Not precisely. More of a happy coincidence."

"Nothing happy about this," I say.

"Well, happiness is relative, isn't it?" the creep replies.

I take a drag, exhale. "I suppose so."

"Now, please, follow me. Quickly. My colleagues are expecting you, and this... incident has compressed our timeline somewhat."

I shake my head, raise my aim to the figure's face. "Before I go any further, I'm going to need a little more explanation."

The shadowy figure grins wide. "Oh, well you're about to help the Bouquet restore justice, peace, and inclusivity for everyone in the Commonwealth. You've been chosen to change this city for the better."

I don't move. Just take another drag.

"And as I previously mentioned, you'll be compensated handsomely, including the PerpetMot upgrades to your synth body," the weasel prattles on. "Upon completion of the important work of protecting this city of the Cap and improving it for generations, of course."

I toss my smoke, holster the gun. "Yeah, okay. Let's check it out."

I cross the street and enter the alley. The shadowy figure grins again, waves his arm at the trash processors and the one on the left slides over, exposing a door. The figure presses his digits against a pad that beeps, flashes orange, then yellow, then green, and pings. The door slides open revealing a small, sterile metal room. Elevator.

"Follow me, Mr. Ono-Marks, to the resistance."

three

As soon as we're on the elevator, the shadowy figure tosses back his hood revealing a bald head, covered in meandering, splotchy scars. Looks like plasma burns. Don't really care how it happened. Just sizing up that he's comfortable enough to be vulnerable. Either that or I'm surrounded with enough defense weaponry that he's actually safe. Given my luck, probably the latter. One of his eyes is synth too. Easy to tell. LED irises flicker because of the refresh rate, always adjusting to minor changes in the light. It's no wonder he saw me from the alley, despite all the CS smoke. Synth eyes'll cut right through that, detect signs of life. Only part I still think about getting, but won't. Gotta keep something of theirs. Mom's eyes. Dad's nose.

The elevator descends and it's clear this isn't some rinkydink op. Light illuminates the shaft, shines through these sliver windows in the carriage. Shadowy figure's synth eye is going bananas, almost looks like it's talking. Convenient because the shadowy figure is talking, giving a little standard exposition on my eager potential partners.

"Welcome to the most secure location in all of the Commonwealth," he says, eyeball wobbling. "I'm Mr. Delta, a field organizer for the Bouquet. The Bouquet operates two distinct arms in its ongoing effort to restore dignity and the right to life for all humans and synths under city jurisdiction. First is the visible facet, the one with which you and most citizens are certainly most familiar. Our opposition government of loyal Bouqs takes action in the Assembly every day to call out the mendacious lies and legislative horrors enacted and supported by the Cap. When they moved to cut pollution regulations in the Undercity, our voices were heard. When they seized citizen-owned structures in the Second, displacing thousands of impoverished Undercitiers, we censured their actions

41

by resolute vote. And when they blocked our request for the Field to extend around the entirety of the Commonwealth, we raised billions in cash to displace their careless, greedy leadership."

I take out another smoke, light it. No lungs, no worries.

"But you didn't actually stop or displace any of them. The Cap is still firmly in charge," I say.

"Not specifically, no," Mr. Delta says. "But the Bouquet has numerous meaningful accomplishments and important contributions decorating its history that you no doubt remember fondly. Anyway, as I was saying: *Those* vocal actors in the Assembly represent the visible facet of the Bouquet. Right now we are entering the invisible facet, the secret heart of the Bouquet, if you will. Our network of covert operatives work tirelessly to undermine the Cap through digital and analog means, whether it's in our 'That's not right!' campaign or more elaborate hackings of Cap data storage. We've even overseen one attempted assassination, which was remarkably successful, save for the assassination part. The important thing is that the Bouquet is working tirelessly to change the Commonwealth for the better, and we're ready to get our hands dirty."

Between the light slipping in and out of the sliver windows and Mr. Delta's talking synth eye, I've stopped paying attention.

"What do you want from me?" I ask.

"Straight to business then," he says. "I like that. But I'm not the person in charge. No. I'll be leading you into the belly of the beast where you can meet our genius leader and she can explain how a freelancer like yourself can contribute to the cause."

"And this cause has the means to pay off my debts and permacharge this tin can."

"Oh it does, and more. You see our donor base comprises dozens of families in the Overcity who've tired of seeing the horrible conditions in the Undercity and want us to create lasting systemic change."

"No market for just giving all that money to folks in the Under, then," I say.

Mr. Delta looks confused. His synth eye dilates, focuses on me. Laughs.

"It's a complicated business, running a city of this size, you see. We can't please everyone, but we must try our very best to find the common grou—"

The elevator lurches. The bald man falls forward. I catch him, push him back to standing.

"Pardon me," he says. "Well then, here we are."

Door slides open onto a brightly lit bullpen of screens, teenagers and twentysomethings with Overcity trashcore haircuts working them, call chatter, awkward urgent running. No windows and plants everywhere, lights must be growers. Wallmount screens show Bouq political posters, slogans:

If not now, when? o

Together we'll try. o

Tomorrow can be today! o

One person can't make a difference, but united, we'll take responsible steps towards change.o

Inspiring stuff. Overhear one kid talking say, "Policy discrepancies between writing and execution are normal, and we have comprehensive data showing that the impact is minimal." Another says, "Don't count the Bouqs out, ma'am. They're counting on the support of multi-racial pro-business individuals who tire of the Cap's antics just like you." There's a main screen on the wall, ten meters across, with a map of the Commonwealth, some sectors colored in gradients of purple and others green. Green must mean the Cap districts of the Overcity. Purple the Bouq districts.

Waypoints speckle it, targets. A war game. The majority of waypoints lie in Boheme, upscale artsy, hipster section of the Over. Target the sympathetics. Beside it, a smaller map for the Undercity. All shades of purple. They know they have support from Undercitiers. What else can we do?

The room stinks of takeout, broth, noodles, inexpensive meat, and time. Dampness too, downside of being underground, however far down we are. The bald guy leads me through the melee taking mini meetings along the way. "I've got the water report from the Third. We improved quality by zero zero zero three percent!" "Mr. Delta, I've just obtained a pledge for C10,000!" Mr. Delta offers fatherly nods, high fives for the donation pledge. "I'll be back for the afternoon huddle in fifteen minutes," he says. "After I deliver this VIP." That draws attention. None worrisome. These kids aren't running in the Commonwealths seedier circles. They're slumming by taking gigs in the Under. Under the Under. I take out another smoke, fire it up. "Excuse me, but you can't do that down here." I wave my hand. "VIP," I say. The kid moves along.

Mr. Delta leads me out of the bullpen down a long corridor. Stainless steel walls and doors. Some open.

Most closed. Same chatter. Fundraising. Policy talk. Distant yelling getting louder as we walk.

"Our volunteer corps is hard at work today as every day," Mr. Delta says, synth eye still wobbling. "And our executives, in these offices, are coordinating numerous campaigns simultaneously to ensure that the volunteers are busy and that the Bouq gets every bit of support it can."

Can't help it. I laugh. And that stops Mr. Delta in his tracks.

"Do you find something humorous about a revolution?" he asks.

Shake my head. "No. Just expected something different. People choking on the air in the Under, working for nothing. Figured your resistance would look a little more rugged."

Mr. Delta scoffs. "Well, it's not my resistance. It belongs to all of us. And the contribution you could make is truly... astounding. But I mustn't spoil it. Here we are."

We reach the source of the yelling. Door's open. A big office, fish tanks, cherry desk in the center, tasteful decor. No posters, no maps. The boss lives here. A real boss. Like the corporate heads or the syndicate types. Cigar smoking, cheek chomping.

She's serious too, screaming on the call, pacing. One of her arms is synth. Hand at least. Dressed like a guerilla with a business jacket.

"I don't care who you have to fuck to get it done, Rho. Get it fucking done! I want so much pressure applied to those Cap assemblypersons that their great-great-grandchildren are filling out forms. No, not literally. Make them fucking hurt!" She ends the call and falls back into the big plush leather chair behind the desk. "I swear on the Articles, Delta, some of these children couldn't open a box of pokkin without step-by-step instructions. How difficult is it to get these Bouq assemblymembers' on message? Honestly! We need to come out of this session looking like we're fighting for the Under. It's not hard. Pollution. Pay. Purpose. Pollution! Pay! Purpose!"

Mr. Delta mouths the words as she says them. Otherwise, just nods until the boss's eyes go wide.

"Silly me. Delta, why didn't you announce yourselves?" she says. "You must be Mr. Ono-Marks. I'm Harriet Alpha, leader of the Bouquet's Underground Resistance and Revolutionary Affairs Office. Welcome to the BURRAO. You must be curious about why I've summoned you here."

"Burrow? Makes you a bunch of moles, then?" I say.

Harriet Alpha laughs. "That's good. And accurate. We *are* the covert faction." She keeps laughing.

"What is it you need from me?" I interject. "And what is it exactly that you're offering?"

The laughter stops abruptly, stagelike. "Mr. Ono-Marks, we need someone with your unique capacities to strike a true blow against the Cap headquarters. And in return for such an act of love for the Bouquet and the People of the Commonwealth whom we hold dear, we are willing to compensate you. It will be more than adequate to free you from your debtors, and set you on the very same path to happiness that your fellow citizens will enjoy once the Cap's influence is stricken from this fair city."

Mr. Delta shuffles around the desk, leans into Harriet Alpha's ear, whispers something that lights her face up.

"And we are prepared to provide you with PerpetMot brand perpetual motion upgrades to your synth... appendages. We have it on corporate authority that this year's line is more efficient than ever, and requires ten percent less maintenance to operate within the optimum band. Honestly, I've been considering getting some synth parts of my own just to try these out. They are truly top of the line."

I nod. "I've seen the holos along the Loop."

"Good. Yes. You would be discerning, given your situation... Which is, of course, beautiful and worthy of honor. Do you prefer to be called a synthetic-humanoid or has that term already gone out of style?"

"My name is fine."

Harriet Alpha nods. "Of course. Very good. Now, I have a couple of short psychological examinations that I'd like you to fill out. You understand that we can't bring an unstable element into the resistance. Matter of fact, we'd prefer to engage the best of the best, regardless of the usual bounds of pedigree."

I hold my hand up. "What's the job?"

She chuckles. Nervous. "The tests can wait. Good." She taps at the screen on her desk. A holo projector pop up, displays a holo of the Cap headquarters. "You'll be infiltrating Cap headquarters to plant a specially-designed EMP device that will eradicate all data and records in their system. This will be designed to look like an accident, which is why we need someone who is neither publicly attached to the Bouquet, nor possesses a background in civic action. Once the device is detonated, the Cap will be crippled and the Bouquet will swoop in to take up the slack left in their wake... after two or three days of fallout come to pass, for obvious reasons. When we take control over governance in the Commonwealth, we can finally end obstruction and clamp down on corporate abuses, air pollution in the Undercity, and rein in the wealth disparities that are punishing tens of millions. We also intend to extend much needed aid to those poor, misled Noncons out in the Wastes. Perhaps we can even fold them back in—"

"So I get into Cap HQ and plant an EMP? Aren't they going to wonder why I'm there?" I say.

Harriet Alpha laughs again. "Yes. Well, we have holobadges to get you inside. We believe you'll be convincing as a custodial engineer. You'll gain access via the service entrance and find your way to the data room from there."

"I'm sure everything will go just like you planned."

Harriet Alpha doesn't pick up on sarcasm. Smiles. "Good! Then I suppose we'll have you sit down and fill out these tests. They should only take about forty-five min—"

"Not doing them," I say. "You want me, we work my way. I'll do your job. You give me half the cash upfront, the other on completion. And I get the PerpetMot upgrade before we start."

She lowers her eyes, frowns. "I'm afraid we can't provide the upgrades first, but I assure you on the honor of the Bouquet that you will receive them. In fact, let me show you something." She taps at her desk screen again and produces another holo. Synth parts, by PerpetMot, floating in a schematic. Then lab test footage. Timelapsed. Synth legs running at fifty klicks per hour for thirty days straight. No cuts. Synth arms doing pushups for ninety days. No cuts. Synth organs pulsing at capacity. One hundred twenty days. No cuts. The real deal. Even if PerpetMot did edit the feed, the parts are luxury. Three tiers above what I've got. Impossible to pass up. Time and money saved. Life on my terms. See Akari less, only downside. Harriet Alpha deactivates the holo, steps around the desk. "I want to be sincere with you, Mr. Ono-Marks. We need you. You are our best and only hope to returning some sense of normalcy and compassion to the Commonwealth. We are prepared to pay you handsomely and as a gesture—" she waves her hand at Mr. Delta "—we have just now transferred C5,000,000 to your name. However, you have illuminated a reasonable concern of risk for both parties in our arrangement. As such, I propose an initial opportunity by which we can build trust."

I nod. That cash'll hold off the corps, cover charges for a while. "Fair enough."

"We have a contact in the Overcity with experience in corporate militia and hacking," Harriet Alpha says. "While we don't have reason to mistrust her, we don't have reason not to at this time. I propose that you meet up with this contact and assist her in an important funding transfer mission."

"I test her, she tests me. Convenient," I say.

Harriet Alpha nods. "Quite. Now, if you're amenable, Mr. Delta will provide you with a miniholo to locate the contact. Once the transfer is complete, we'll be able to formalize our partnership and land the killing blow on the Caps!"

I nod. Harriet Alpha smiles. We shake hands. Old customs. Mr. Delta leads me out of the office, back down the corridor, through the bullpen, back into the elevator. As we ride up, he places the miniholo in my hand. I activate it. The Contact is who I'd expect. No name given. Pretty, shimmer-haired, mousy and unassuming, smart. Dossier's long. Hacking. Cash fraud. ID fabbing. All techcrimes. Save for one assault. Knifed a chud in a club in the Over. Served ten days for it. Chud lived. Tried to rape her. Offset part of the sentence. Funny system we got. Punishing the punished. Contact is dangerous for those reasons and more. Might be a setup, but C5,000,000 richer means it's a chance worth taking. That, and living permacharge'd change everything. Could wander the Wastes, try to get out of the Commonwealth altogether. I pocket the miniholo as the elevator settles up top. Mr. Delta's wobbling synth eye bids me farewell and I step out onto the Undercity street. Just me, sanitation mechs, and the holo-splash smog to light my way back to the Kento.

four

Two p.m. in the Overcity Center. Been away so long my eyes barely adjust to the sunlight streaming through the Field. All the mirrored glass buildings don't help. Like living inside a laser. Shades set to Max. Should be fine but still seeing spots. Miniholo on the Kento's dash shows the Contact. Supposed to meet her inside a dayclub called GaGa's. Forgot the kinds of freetime Overcitiers have for dayclubs, rental parks, joyriding. Sidewalks up here are abuzz with folks with nothing to do and all the time in the world to do it in. On calls, walking with screens, pets. Corporates too, mostly zecs, suited, waving their arms with import, sitting on terraces with their own. All under blue skies, with grassy patches and fields, and trees. Lots of trees. Some of them holo, but this section of the Over was reforested a few years back, big Cap project to replace the old pixelated holos with GMOs that thrive under the Field, even shave off 0.09% of emissions going to the under through the root system. Genius, for those who deserve it.

I drive carefully, casually. Nothing cute up here. One thing to get caught in the Loop, but the corporate cops up here don't do bribes and they don't treat Undercitiers well. Fact that I've got a record at all, hell even just the debt, is enough for Overcity cops. Liable to impound the Kento before asking me a question. Traffic's bad too. Nothing wider than two lanes in the Over. Claimed the rest for greenbelts, walking plazas. Easy enough when no one has to be anywhere at any particular time. Of course, I do, but I'm not the audience. Sit behind a brand new Solaris X10, lifted, Wasteland package, clean and pristine. Kid inside doesn't even clear the headrest. Reminds me of the first time I drove with Dad, I'm holding the wheel, he's working the pedals, telling me when to shift, helping me. Did a quick five laps in the Wastes, just so I could get the feel. I was ten, I think.

Miniholo starts chirping. GaGa's is close. Yep. Up on the left about a block. I shut the miniholo down, slip it into my jacket pocket, wait for an opening and then pull over into a parking column. Maglifts carry me and the Kento up ten, twenty, fifty stories, slide over and deposit us in an available autocabin. "Thank you for choosing FamilyTech Parking Services. Complete face scan at the screen to begin payment and activate the exit elevator." Pop the gullwing on the Kento, slip out and lock it up. Pat myself down, check my leg holster. All good if there's trouble. I approach the branded screen, still of a happy Overcity family keeps it occupied while it waits for me. Eye over the screen opens, bathes me in green light. One pass, brow to chin. Second pass, ear to ear. "Hello, Run Ono-Marks. Your vehicle is in good hands. C300 will debit from your account for each hour, not to exceed C2100. FamilyTech Parking Services appreciates your business. Enjoy your day!" Just outside the autocabin another maglift appears, human-sized. The safety barrier opens, I step through, and watch the Kento disappear into a tiny speck as I descend fifty-some stories, nearly weightless.

At ground level, maglift chimes, I exit. Couple of joggers with exercise-augments fly by me. Faster than the traffic. Must be nice to have the synth experience without the sacrifice. Lots of things must be nice. Get to the corner and cross the street with the signal. Everything carefully here. Everything. GaGa's is a big chrome building shaped like a blooming flower. Holos splash all over it, dulling the shine a bit, reminding folks what the day's specials are, who's coming to the Commonwealth for a special appearance or show. No bouncers or enforcers at the door up here. Wouldn't be for the night shift either. Just facerec all around the aural disrupted entrance. Get scanned on entry. No alarms. No attention. Soon as I cross the threshold, I hear the music. Bouncing, looping dayclub shit. Sunnier than the blinding outdoors. Mobile holos fly around the vaulted ceiling, spinning neons and throwing colors and shapes all around the room. One second folks look blue. Next they look pink. Back and forth. Eyes adjust quickly. I tuck my shades away and start looking for the Contact.

Center of GaGa's is a sprawling dancefloor with maglift tiers allowing for four levels of dancing on air. Around the outside's all cafe tables, each with its own service screen, dispenser, and aural limiting to keep folks from yelling over the music. Crowded joint for two-something in the afternoon, but that's what dayclubs are for. Clientele is a mix of the same as outside. Some corporate zecs at the cafe tables, mostly hitting on dancing crowd, plying them with drinks, trying to draw them back to private offices for midday toma. Dancers writhing and crashing and humping each other on the floor and in the air above among the hovering holos. All dayclub wear, racersuits, jumpers, tees and short shorts. Air smells of liquor, lightdrugs and vape. Crossing the floor I get grabbed everywhere, everyway, by everyone. Synth parts mute the sensations that need to be, keep me from getting distracted. Push through the bouncing bodies, snag the maglift up to the second tier, and drop my hood.

I scan the room quickly, HUD tries to match the woman in the miniholo with anyone in the club. Panning, it's a mess. Dancers on this tier keep bouncing in the way, phasing from down below or up above. Finally, HUD IDs her, corner table in the back, sitting with her profile to the door. Tall martini glass in front of her. Miniholo in her hand with my face flickering on it. Stupid. I descend the maglift, removing my hood at the same time, and stroll through the mess of humanity. From five meters away it's definitely her. Pretty, shimmer-haired, mousy and unassuming, smart. Shimmer-hair keeps catching the hololights, seems to go clear for a moment, tricks.

"Waiting for me?" I say, stepping up to her table.

Head stays still, shimmer-hair glows blue, purple, red, orange. "Take a hike. I don't fuck with zecs."

"I'm no zec," I say. Take out the miniholo, activate it, set it on the center of the table. "And you're no dayclubber."

Eyes slide over to me, face half turns. Shimmer-hair goes platinum. "Sit down," she says. "Order something. Look like we're friends or we're gonna fuck."

I oblige. Service screen lists food, bevs, lightdrugs, song requests. Page through, order a whiskey soda with lime, basket of breaded meat-sub fingers extra spicy. Screen slaps the items on the bill listed at the center of the table. Dispenser starts humming, chimes. **Order Complete. Please Remove Items**. I open the bin. Inside on a tray, my drink in a sealed dissolvable capsule suspended over an empty glass, the meat-sub fingers in a heat pod, sauce connected like a sidecar. Pull out the tray, set it on the table. The Contact goes straight for the fingers, pops the pod and it sizzles, heat rushing out. Pours half the sauce over the pod, sets the other half aside. Doesn't wait for me a second. I give the whiskey soda capsule a shake, crack it on the edge of the table, pour it into the glass. In the bottom of the glass, the dehydrated lime wedge swells, taking on some of the drink.

"So, you're who the Bouqs send?" the Contact says, mouthful of meat-sub.

"Same as you, I suppose," I say, sipping.

She coughs. "We're not the same. The Bouqs don't send me. They send to me." Then she grabs my free arm, starts stroking it. Laughs big and fake. Runs her finger down into my palm and starts drawing donuts. "Laugh, idiot. There's UC militia in here doing security. That one, in the white jumper just looked at us."

Sure enough. Tons of them, all wearing the same white jumper with pink and gold piping. How dumb can you be, going undercover in uniforms? I clock the UCs in my sightline. Just circling from table to table. Pausing, listening in, touching comms on their lapels, mumbling, moving on. Drug detail more than likely. Maybe prostitution. They aren't here to stop it, just want to get the club's cut of anything juicy, ensure it's kept quiet enough to avoid big trouble.

I look at the Contact, pin a big, dumb grin on my face. Grin of an Overcitier with dayclubbing cash. I laugh. Haven't in a while. Feels strange. Take her hand and entwine our fingers, start smiling like I'm closing a date. "I'm just here for the job," I say quietly.

Presence hovers behind us. The UC. It lingers.

Contact leans across the table, cheek to cheek, lips on left ear. "I've got a job for you," she says, tongue swirling. "Later, but let's finish eating and have a dance first, darling. This beat gets me in the mood." She says it loud, too loud to not be heard. Pulls me in close by my jacket lapel, plants one on me.

Haven't been kissed since, don't even remember exactly. Last partner I had was before I hocked my legs, lungs, heart. Contact really goes for it. Tongue, suction. A good actress. Good enough. The UC militia buys it, putters away from us and buzzes over toward another table. Contact leans back in her seat, face stays romantic, everything else goes full professional. "Don't get any ideas," she says.

"Fresh out," I say.

"Very smart. Here's the deal," stilted, mechanical, and smiling all the way. "I'm the firewall. You don't get in good with the Bouqs until you go through me. Translation: I own you starting the moment you stepped into this club. You don't think for yourself. You don't make plans. You don't have concerns unless I raise them. You don't pull a piece or land a punch unless I say so. And you don't ask questions. If there's something you need to know, you'll know it, and if there's something you don't know—"

"Then I don't need to know it."

Contact grimaces. "Too cute. I don't care for predictive types."

"Mind if I have a smoke? Or does that qualify as a question?"

She waves her hand in irritated approval.

I lean over to the service screen, activate the ventilator. Ashtube pops out of the center of the table, starts sucking air outside. Light up, take a drag, blow a plume into the vent, watch it slither away. Look at the Contact silently.

"You're going to do a pick up for me, and if you do a fine enough job I'll vouch for you with the Bouqs," she says. "It should be simple for someone with your resume. It's a cash terminal. I'll give you the hackkey. It's got cash transport tech credentials built in, so try to look professional. Then all you have to do is login, make a couple transfers, one to the Bouqs, one to me. Terminal location and both transfer addresses are on the key. Then you just logout and walk away looking like a real nobody who's on the up and up, moving along to do another fuckall . I'll be watching so don't be creative. Seriously. Fuck around and find out." Her eyes underline the seriousness. Then she quickly glances over my right shoulder, smiles wide again, licks her lips aggressively enough to have taken them right off.

I wink in acknowledgement.

Another UC militia saunters past us. They must have our scent. Contact picks it up too, pays the table, leans in close again, lips puckered.

"The hackkey is in my left breast pocket," she continues. "We're going to get up and dance. You're going to grab my ass. Then you're going to kiss me. Then you're going to feel me up. Those synth fingers better be nimble, because you need to nick that hackkey and pocket it. Then you kiss me some more, we finish the dance, and get out of here."

I nod, let the smoke fall from my fingers into the ashtube. Gone. Stand up and offer my hand like a real regal gentleman of days gone. She takes it, stands, beams at me. Lead her to the dance floor, find a clear spot among the chaotic swirl of flesh, find the beat. Contact dances in close to me, grinds up on my left thigh, mouths, "Now." I reach around, grab her ass with one hand, pull her in tight, plant one on her, and send my hand up to her breast pocket. Up and under, feel her up like she said, detect the hackkey, slide it over. Gotta move it sideways out the vertical zipper toward the middle of the shirt, makes for a convincing grope. Keep kissing her. She keeps grooving on me, has one hand holding the hand on her ass, the other on the back of my head. We might be good dancers. Hackkey drops between synth index and thumb. I flip it down, into my palm, press and slide it into the jacket sleeve. Open the compartment in my forearm, let the key drop in, locked and safe. I say, "Yes" into her open mouth. She removes my hand from her ass, entwines our fingers, then lets go. Still kissing. Does the same with the other hand. Breaks the kiss, gives me a come here motion and walks off the floor toward the door. I pause, smile like a lovestruck schooler, and follow her out.

Hackkey's got an old messenger log embedded. When I link it to the screen on the Kento, it retrieves a static gridmap. Older tech, but functional. Gridmap highlights the Data Records level of the CommonCash Bank campus. Happens to be in a nice part of the Over. Neighborhood called Eden. Nicer than where I used to be by far. Zecs and owners, generationals and celebs. Eden is where old cash and new cash come together to drink to living without worry. All the towers are self-contained new urban bastions. The parks are gated. Whole place is patrolled by drones with full extrajudicial auth. Comes up on the newsfeed now and again, drone'll have blown away a bird or a stray dog caught nesting or digging. Worst case was when a NonCon was sneaking food out via Eden's private city access door. Three drones surrounded him, while three more recorded. Horrific shit even with the pixelation they use on the feed.

Drop my jacket in the trunk of the Kento, pop the panel on my left arm, and activate incog. It'll eat charge but it's the only way this is going to work. Synth parts project a cash transport tech uni from every pore node. In a second I look like I work for CommonCash, as long as you don't look too close, or grab at me. Should get me through the security around Eden. Walk back and start climbing back into the Kento. Stop to look around. She said she's watching. Wonder if that includes right now. Pull down the gullwing and wait for the FamilyTech popup onscreen. Two taps, `disengage, yes I'm pleased with my parking experience`. My spot slides out on maglifts, lowers from the column to street level. One more message: `Have a terrific FamilyTech day!`

Drive to Eden takes thirty minutes. Traffic is light this time of day. Overcitiers are back at work or thoroughly entrenched in dayclubs, other activities. Eden's got a garish holo at its entrance. I queue up behind the other cars looking to get in. The holo runs a little story about how the neighborhood was founded, all fiction, of course, but with enough cash you write the history you like. Starts with a family literally climbing out of the Undercity, dressed in tattered rags, wet, dirty. On ascent, they move through decades of Commonwealth architecture. Early brutalist stuff, modern, classic revival, neofunctional, technophilic, etc. At the top of the ladder, the man helps the woman and children up then they look out over untouched verdant fields. Complete bullshit. Spontaneously the family members smile, nod at each other. Then poof, family's all cleaned up, new clothes, healthy. And then towers with terraces, shopping, offices, homes, interior and exterior parks, built-in ag, exercise tubes and treads, delivery hubs, AI concierge... everything. And more and more towers grow up out of the ground, until the whole field is full of them. Family shares an exaggerated hug and the kids run into one of the towers. Parents follow just behind. `Welcome to Eden. Paradise in the Commonwealth.`

Queue moves fast enough. I pull the Kento up to the gate, turn on the credentials in the hackkey. Four drones buzz around, scanning. Takes a couple passes, then I'm cleared. Drones wave me along. Not much to see between the gate and the CommonCash campus. Edenites appear mostly in their towers. From street level, only those without digishades let you peek inside. A couple zecs working over a tablescreen on floor two. Yoga class ten stories up. Flashes from a giant screen on twenty-four. Dancing silhouettes on thiry-nine. Shoppers on fifty to seventy-eight. Still green in the eighties. Must be gardens or ag. Outside, some joggers. Folks walking their dogs. Nothing exciting. Eden's a boring place. You pay a whole hell of a lot to be so comfortably bored.

Follow the gridmap to the CommonCash campus. Sprawling compound with holos dedicated to cash creating more cash creating happiness. Pull up to the parking tower, flash the creds again. Kento gets lifted to an employee deck, slid right into a reserved spot beside the staff lift. Lock the Kento, slip the hackkey into my arm compartment. A couple of CommonCash employees, tellers probably, based on the dress, pop out from the maglift when it arrives. "What a day. I can't believe how well you're doing for bonus this week! It's not even fair. I can never get new accounts." "It's all about persistence. Make sure they know that you're thinking about them and their plans for the future. Then you just have to show them the way to make those dreams come true with CommonCash products." "That's genius, you know." "It's not genius. It's just human connection." If I still had a stomach, I'd vomit. Give the two CommonCash mooks a knowing nod and slip past into the lift. Halfway down, a couple well-dressed zecs hop in, talk about development ops in the Under. "It'll never work. No one wants to be down there." "But I'm thinking it's an experience. No one's ever tried to sell the slums before. Who needs gentrification if you can sell that gritty mundanity for more than the new stuff?" "I don't buy it." They get off at the conference center bridge. Six more levels and I step off at Data Records.

From the maglift, step into a clean room. Evapchem shoots all over me, smells like alcohol and rose scent. Incog goes static for a sec. Hold my breath. Worst place to get found out. Green light and a chime, keep walking. After the clean room, four-stage auth gates stand between me and Data Records. Walk casual through each, flashing the hackkey. No trouble until the third gate. Returns a fatal error, reboots. Cams pop down from the ceiling, out of the walls. Comm clicks loudly. "Hey, sorry about this. We've been having issues with the new patch. Give me a couple minutes to get the system back online."

I look one of the cams straight on. "Zecs breathing down my neck about productivity. You know how it is. Just have a couple quick transfers to make. I can't get behind or I'll miss out on bonus. Cut me some slack this time?" Flash the teeth.

Silence for a moment. Intolerably long. Keep smiling. Comm clicks on again.

"I hear you, pal. I've been worried this patch issue will cost me bonus too. Go ahead and be quick. If anyone asks, you got in there clear, before the system crashed. Okay?"

Hold up a thumb. "Of course, friend," I say. "Thanks for helping out. If you ever need anything, look me up." I flash the hackkey creds at the cam, grin once more for good measure. "Thanks again."

Data Records is dozens and dozens of aisles of servers, private-leased data safes, and cash terminals. Luckily, everything's labeled. Corps are good for that, lots of structure, lots of idiot-proofing. I take the row labeled Cash Terminals - Authorized Transport Technicians Only. Hackkey messenger log shows AA253. Second layer. Great. Couldn't be right by the exit, could it? Pass the first twenty-six terminal stacks, stand at AA, scan for 253. Numbers aren't in order left to right, top to bottom. Finally, there it is. AA253. Insert the hackkey, watch the screen boot and read. Look down both directions. Still alone. Welcome back, Martin Lindwell. splashes onscreen. Then a button reading Delete Recent Transport Record.

Then buttons for the two transfers: Initiate Fund Transport to JJ:828:UCX101 and Initiate Fund Transport to [Info Redacted]. First one must be the Contact, second one is the Bouqs, or whoever it is. No point in redacting a transport location when neither human nor synth can read them. That code cypher is proprietary to CommonCash, so they'd be the only ones who could read it, if the hackkey wasn't going to erase the record. Hiding that information from me, maybe even the Contact. Makes sense. The

Bouqs probably see their fair share of retributive action, dealing with types like me.

Tap the button to start the transport to the Contact. If she's really watching, she'll appreciate that i'm not putting her second. Signs of allegiance can go a long way. Screen reads: **Transport Initiated**, and the time bar fills from left to right. After a few moments, the bar is full and the initial screen reloads. I tap **Initiate Fund Transport to [Info Redacted]** and again, a time bar appears, filling more slowly. A lot more slowly. That's when I hear the door to Data Records open with a dull whoosh, sound of boot heels, three, no, four pair. CommonCash doesn't have their own militia, so these must be hired hands. Boots stop. I'm in trouble. They wouldn't be here if the disguise worked. Shit.

"You, check the servers," some corp militia barks. "You two, secure the data safes. I'll checkout the cash terminals. Keep your comms active. No surprises." Then the boots clamber again.

Take a deep breath. Activate the cloak and press myself up against the BB cash terminal. From the corner of my eye, watch the time bar slowly fill. Twenty percent. Come on. At the end of the aisle, there he is. PalCorp, black and purple ballistic armor, shock helmet, T-18 multi-function blaster rifle. Starting to think I've been set up. The security monitor outside Data Records was too easy, too helpful. Intentionally so. PalCorp soldier peers down the aisle, looking for me, checks between each terminal, looking for someone stupid enough to wedge themselves among them, hopefully not thinking about someone stupid enough to go invis and just stand there. Look at the terminal again, forty percent. PalCorp keeps moving my way, waving his rifle around like a kid playing at it. His comm lights up. "Chief, looks like we're all clear in servers. Nothing out of place. Orders?" "Good. Swing back around and join me in Cash Terminals," Chief says. "I don't see anything here yet, still completing my sweep. The extra set of eyes will help." Chief stops in his tracks, somewhere around stacks Q and R. He's going to wait? Exhale slowly, check the screen. Sixty-five percent. Gotta stay still. Cloak won't be worth shit in a tight space like this if I start moving. Cham-lag'll give me away. I'll flicker like someone dancing on the third maglevel of GaGa's. Shock of haptic feedback nearly throws me forward. Look at my forearm. Fuck. I know this alert. Warning: Charge Level at 20%! Discontinue Auxiliary Systems to Preserve

Essential Operations. Stupid. Should've thought of that. Can't run incog and cloak back to back. Too much drain. Just need a couple minutes more. Finish the transport, get out of here, straight to Akari's.

Second PalCorp soldier sidles up by the Chief. Two of them continue down the aisle. S. T. U. V. Check the screen. Eighty-two percent. This better finish before they see the screen lit up. Soldiers keep walking. W. X. Y. Charge meter on my arm reads 18%. Screen reads ninety-six percent. Sweat on my brow. Nowhere else. Can't sweat anywhere else anymore. PalCorp at Z. "Chief, that terminal look activated to you?" soldier asks. "Sure does. Good eye. We've got a rat," the Chief says, starts reaching for his comm to contact the other two on patrol. On screen: **ninety-eight percent**. The other soldier reaches for the terminal, fingers hovering over the inserted hackkey.

And I wanted this to be quiet, easy. I pop a blade from my synth hand, slash down on the soldiers fingers as they reach for the hackkey, slice them all off at the second knuckle. Soldier yelps, stumbles back, drops his rifle. On screen: **Transport Complete. Tap Exit. Screen reads: Thank you, Martin Lindwell. Have a pleasant day!** I pull the hackkey free, slide it into my forearm compartment. Chief

73

whips around. Sees me flickering. "You! Stop!" Trains his rifle on me. I charge at him, blades out of both synth hands. Two slashes. Rifle fires. Blast catches me in the stomach. I smell melting. System struggles to seal the shot. Nanos start flowing to the damage. 12% charge remaining. In front of me, Chief coughs, head tips back revealing both slashes across his throat. Drops his gun, grabs the wound as if it'll matter, collapses. Blood everywhere. I leap over Chief and wounded soldier, sprint down to the entrance, hear "What was that?" echo from the data safes aisle. Boot clatter. They're on their way. I kill the cloak and the incog. Just a mostly nude synth with a blast scar in his stomach, running. Nothing to worry about.

Beat them to the door, but they're right behind. "Hey! Stop where you are. PalCorp militia has authority here!"

I do not obey. Keep running, full speed, fifty-five clicks per hour, straight through the four security gates. Alarms sound. Comm lights up. "Nice try, asshole," my friend says. "You won't outrun the drones." Watch me. Keep moving. Clean room tries to spray me on the way out, can't keep up. Sprinting, drained... slowing down a few klicks. 10% charge. Feeling a little sluggish. Down the bridge toward the maglift. Outside, drones are closing in on the bridge. Can't get me here at least. Wave madly at the sensor. Look back, see the two PalCorp mooks plodding along. Lucky me, lift door opens. It's free and waiting. Hop in, prod the screen for the level the Kento is on, and ride. Fucking thing is slow. Wish there was an override terminal, not that I've got the juice to spare to hack it right now. Outside, drones are tracking me going up. Zecs in an adjacent lift, going down, gawk like idiots as the me and my tail ascend.

Lift finally chimes and stops. Get out and break for the Kento, limping now. 6% charge. Damage Successfully Repaired. Connect Charge Soon. Small favors. Drag my weak ass to the Kento, flop against the gullwing, it opens. Duck down, throw myself into the seat, start it up. Pedal to the floor, tear around on the garage level, skid into the employee parking exit, catching a lift to ferry us down, weakly flash the hackkey creds at the parking scanner. Chimes. Thank you for visiting CommonCash. Exit lift grabs the Kento, starts us down, always too slow. The flock of drones, unloseable, buzz around outside the vehicle lift. Five of them now. All barking commands. Can't make out what they're saying. Too many chattering at once to focus. Weapons clearly charging, bright red light is unmistakable. 3% charge. Losing my breath. Heart slowing down. Feeling tired. No choice now.

Tap at the Kento's screen and turn on Flight Mode. Kento's engine hums and groans, power transfers from the drivetrain to the repulsor jets under the chassis. Car lurches up, roof bumps on the top of the maglift compartment, sizzles against the static field. I activate the Kento's anti-mag field. Supposed to be for getting it out of impound, and it's more than powerful enough to break a maglift. Right when the anti-mag field warms up, the Kento phases out of the lift, lift keeps going down, we stay flying. I catch a break. The drones keep pace with the lift for just a second, so I crank the throttle up to full and stream out of the maglift column, straight through the CommonCash campus, and out into Eden. 2% charge. Not thinking straight. Do I go back to GaGa's? No. No. The Loop. Get to the Loop. Drones catch up, on our tail. Start firing on the Kento. Car shakes with each hit, wobbles, but it's sturdy. Shots splash against the shatterproof rear window, leaving marks, but holding strong. Soar between the lux towers of Eden, toward the holos at the entrance. Right as that fiction family starts to hug, We come blasting through. I crank the wheel, putting the Kento into a spin. Only way to be sure the gate scanners won't read us clean. Pull the Kento up in a nearly vertical climb, catch the angle to cut a clean line through the Overcity straight into the Loop. 1% charge. Lose two of the drones on the climb, engines fail them. They fall back. Push the nose down and barrel toward the Loop, glowing lanes stuffed with cars. Two more drones clip on towers on the way down. Only one more. Still firing. Kento's shaking a lot. Loop's just a couple klicks away.

Fumble with the screen for the sparklers. Hand not working easily. Three slaps later, I find the button. **Engage Countermeasures?** Only measures I got left. Charge gauge flashing. **Entering Survival Mode in 10... 9... 8...** Mash the screen. Behind the Kento a spray of sparks and fireworks shoots out from between the taillights. Drone gets caught up in them, spins out, goes ass-up, tumbles, drops out of the sky. Made it. Too loud though. Not going to be good when they find me. **7... 6... 5...** Kento speeds toward the Loop. I can barely focus. Breaths shallow. Ringing in ears. Eyes closing. Row of Haulers sit in the upper left lane, row of drivers behind them no doubt screaming mad. Try to hit the brake, foot doesn't work. No lift, no limber. Flop my arm on the e-brake, fingers weak, just try to hook it. Pull with what I got left. E-brake gives a bit. Kento tips, pitches, spins. 4... 3... 2... Full tumble. Oh well. Nice knowing me. Haulers coming up fast. Big trucks. Bigger up close. Heading to T-bone. 1... Kento's prox alarm starts screaming. "Vehicle ahead! Vehicle ahead!" Last thing I see's a Hauler driver's terrified face closing in. 0. Survive1 m0∂e$ ∆¢ ███████████████████ 0

five

Rush of energy. Gasping. Awake. Synth heart racing.

Wherever I am it's all white, bright white light. I'm dead. I must be dead. Last thing I remember is the Kento flying full throttle into a hauler. Yeah. I'm dead. Didn't think there was an afterlife. Joke's on me, I guess. At least it's warm. Feels like sunshine. Music's nice too. New acid jazz, maybe? Not quite my heaven, but it ain't hell either.

Light suddenly moves. A lamp. Silhouette of someone, not clear. Stupid human eyes still adjusting. I blink hard. Lift my arms and rub my eyes, as if that'll help.

"Apologies for the blindness." Who's voice is that? "I just finished doing a stress-test diagnostic. You passed with flying colors, though you might feel like you've just run a marathon." I do feel like that. "Don't get up too fast. Give your synth organs a couple more minutes to settle back to normal operating band. After that, get dressed and meet me on the terrace."

Owner of the voice disappears. They're familiar. Recent. I feel my synth heart rev down, synth lungs slow, fuller, deeper breaths. Open my mouth wide, pop my jaw, and sit up. I'm on a table in some lux tower loft. Floor and ceiling are all white, white columns pepper the open room. One wall is all windows, must be the terraces. Lamp above me, like Akari's. Beside the table is a charging station, newer than Akari's, still has protective plastic wrap on the screen and pad. Across the room, a collection of seating around a huge holoprojector, the kind you see in clubs or on newsfeed stories about life in the Over. New acid jazz combo playing on it right now, incredible definition. Really sounds like they're in the room, playing live. Swing my legs over the edge of the table, see my jacket on the chair, undamaged. Or repaired. Not sure yet. I get dressed. Run my own diagnostic. Never trust second opinions. Not even

Akari's. Check comes back clear. No damage, no errors. Repair nanos replenished too. Charge meter reads 100%. Still possible that I'm dead. Pop my arm compartments, hackkey is still inside where I left it, close them. Pop my leg compartment. Iron's gone. Probably not dead after all. Just not my lucky day.

I start toward the bank of windows, spot a sliding glass door, and beyond it, a shimmer-haired woman— the Contact—sitting at a cafe table, holding a mug of something, hitting a vape. Slip through the door, the Contact smiles at me, gestures for me to sit.

"Would you like anything to drink or eat?" she says. Her pleasantness is unsettling.

I take a smoke from my jacket pocket, light up. Drag. Exhale. Drag. Exhale. Look out over the Commonwealth. Quite a view. Klicks and klicks of towers, cars buzzing about the sky, holos floating, bobbing and weaving, newsfeeds showing gruesome NeonCube highlights, footage from Recognition Day. Some sick Under kid, bald and scabby, dressed up nice in FamilyTech's L'il Leader line gets a ceremonial holokey to the Commonwealth from some Cap zecs along with a transfer of C2,500,000 and a living cube for two in the Ambrosia neighborhood. Cap zec says they'll give the kid synth parts to cure whatever disease they've got. "What an honor, on another Recognition Day, to be able to share our success with one of our citizens in need," zec says, touching the kid like they go way back. "As we start the week's celebration, let us all remember that there, but for the Grace of Cap, go we all!" Kid gets to tap on a screen the zec's holding, bunch of holos shaped like balloons appear and fall down around them. Feed changes to another story about the Noncons. Drone footage with a voiceover, like some nature doc. Bunch of ramshackle huts made of car doors, Hauler boxes. A few Noncons huddled around a firepit, looks like a bunch of lizards on a spit slow roasting. "Despite attempts to reach out to the Waste-bound radicals, Commonwealth officials state that the Noncons show no signs of interest even as they continue to expose their children to unsanitary, poisonous conditions. Updates on the hour."

"My gun," I say. "And my car."

The Contact sips from her mug, sets it down, smiles. "Of course. I wasn't sure how you'd handle the charge from zero so I locked your firearm in my safe out of an abundance of caution. As for your vehicle, it is currently being repaired in my garage space, with new registration, of course." She slides another hackkey across the table. "Your Kento is now Navid Francis's Kento, and as far as the Corps are concerned, you are Navid Francis. Run Ono-Marks was killed in the vehicle malfunction that took the lives of three hauler drivers, and destroyed C1,875,000 in HomeCom furnishings. Run Ono-Marks' Kento was obliterated in the collision, along with Run Ono-Marks. Of course, the Commonwealth will still recognize your optic scans and biowave patterns, so your city debts remain intact and connected to your Citizen Number. It's a pity that the Caps really monitor all the municipal systems. The Corps are easy, only worried about the cash, don't care about user data. The Commonwealth has to look like they serve a higher purpose."

"I'd like a whiskey now," I say.

The Contact touches the screen on the cafe table and a whiskey pops up out of its center, just like at GaGa's, a pod with a glass. I crack it, slug the booze back. Tap on the table. The Contact pours me another.

"Before you ask, I said I would be watching you, and I was. You did a fine job, Run. Transports went off just fine, and I'm honestly very impressed that you stuck it out until the one for the Bouqs completed." She hits her vape, laughs. "I know I wouldn't have."

"What the fuck happened?" I ask.

She raises an eyebrow, shimmer-hair changes from pink to yellow to green. "Someone hacked on Comm, put a tap in. They knew exactly what you were doing from the moment we spoke. I couldn't understand it. Those mooks at GaGa's weren't tapping us. But when I started the repair program on your Kento, I found an encoded bug. Must've been on the hackkey."

"One of the Bouqs."

The Contact nods. "Either someone there doesn't source their hackkeys well, or they tapped this one on purpose. CommonCash was reading it the whole time, knew your cover story, and once you linked it to your car, they knew where you were."

I hold up the hackkey with Navid Francis's ID on it. Inspect it.

"I triple checked that one myself. It was clean before I loaded the identity files," she says. "I don't make second mistakes. Problem is that whoever tapped that key is still probably dealing with the Bouqs, and that means we have an ongoing vulnerability."

I slug the second whiskey. "And?"

The Contact looks down into her mug, lifts those big, beautiful eyes up. "And I'd like you to help me take care of it."

I laugh. Feels good. "Seems to me I was proving myself to some folks who couldn't even prove themselves, and that leaves me feeling reluctant about a continuation of the partnership."

She nods. Shimmer-hair shifts from green to blue to purple. "The thing is, dealing with this complication is beneficial for all parties. The Bouqs get rid of an antagonizing operative. I get the peace of mind of knowing that records of my participation, and my personal information return to their essential, fully obfuscated standards. And you, Run, have the opportunity to fulfill the job you agreed to, for the rewards due, including a body that will no longer fail you in the midst of a violent high speed chase, requiring hours of Overcity surveillance hacking, CommonCash and PalCorp record revision, three dead bystanders, two days of vehicle repairs, a new life, and a nearly failed trip to the recharge table."

I tap the table again. "One more."

"So early in the day?" she says. "You *were* just resurrected."

Another whiskey pops out. I take it, crack it, have a sip. "Suppose I just take Navid Francis's life and car and get out of here, don't look back?"

"You could try, Run. But I can erase the record on that hackkey whenever I want, couldn't I?" she says. "What I was trying to express is that your continued participation is a win-win-win scenario, and I think you'll be a lot happier if you start thinking about it that way. You won't be doing this for the Bouqs. Hell, I don't trust the Bouqs a micron. They talk a good game. They have some inspiring words. But they're just like any of the Corps. Just like the Caps. Anything that gets so big as to see itself as a way of life, as the proper solution is ripe and ready to fuck anybody who gets in its way. You think that the political theater they act in day in and day out has anything to do with making this city better?" She laughs. "It's to keep people looking, keep them tied up in the conflict. Make them believe there's good guys and bad guys. Truth is, there's only bad guys, all of us riding a spectrum from kiddie fucker to bread thief. You and me, we're much closer to bread thief. The Bouqs, the Caps, the Corps. They're all kiddie fuckers because they let the system fuck kids while they make excuses for why it's just how it is. You're not working for

86

them. You're doing it for yourself, and to an extent for me."

"I don't even know who you are," I say.

Her face softens. "You want to know who I am? How do you know that I even know who I am anymore?"

"You must call yourself something," I say. "'The Contact' lacks both flair and gravitas."

Her eyes widen. "You're not the usual merc the Bouq deals with."

"'Cause I said 'gravitas'?" I ask.

"That, and I figured you'd have either been gung ho about the money, revenge, that sort of thing, or you'd have forced me to sic my security measures on you," she says. "You've done neither."

I spark another smoke. "Yeah. I'm full of surprises. Used to live near here. Elysium. Lifetime ago."

"You're an Overcitier?" she asks.

"Was. Parents died. Bills piled up. Had to move to the Under. Sell everything."

Her shimmer-hair turns warm gold. "Sounds like a tough life. I lost my parents too."

"That right?" I ask.

"Mostly," she says. "They got real involved with the Cap after the Noncons left. Said it was a terrorist act to disrupt our way of life. Disowned me when I told them I liked a couple of those ideas. Tried to kick me down to the Under, but I hacked every record and key here, got them kicked out. They tried to fight me on it, but turns out you don't want to take your kid before the magistrate when it looks like you've been napping Undercity children to use as models for fuckbots. They don't talk to me anymore."

"Can't say I blame them," I say.

She nods. "It's for the best. I don't need any heartless joiners in my life. Anyone who'd go along with what the Caps say, or the Bouqs, even the Noncons, with that much blind dedication isn't... well, I have a feeling you know what I mean and I can save the rant."

"In fact, I do. Funny thing about selling your major organs and body parts to pay the bills, one tends to lose faith in his fellow humans."

The Contact stands up from the cafe table and walks over to the terrace railing. Stares off into space for a moment, sighs, shakes her head, turns back toward me. "I'll probably regret this later, but I have a deal for you."

Sip my drink, take a drag. "I'm listening."

"You agree to help me take care of the Bouq who bugged our hackkey, and I'll tell you my name," the Contact says.

I blink. "I'll never know if it's your real name," I say. "And from the sound of things, you could've hacked away any records of it if it was." I grin.

She rolls her eyes, sits back down at the table, raps her fingers, shimmer-hair falls across her face, glows iridescent blue. "Fine. I'll throw in another C1,000,000 from my transfer, as a sign of good faith. I want you to know you can trust me," she says.

Another million would be nice. Buy me a way out of the Commonwealth once the debt's repaid. Finally be a free man, not like before when I was tethered to the Over, not like now when I'm tethered to the Under, the weekly charges. Start thinking about taking the Kento through the Wastes, tearing around on open ground, running across other cities, new jobs, maybe there's even a place where they figured out how not to fuck it all up. Probably not, but a boy can dream.

"I'll do it," I say. "But you don't send me that mil until after it's done. If we're doing a trust deal, we'll do it even."

Her eyes light up. "Even a man of principles. Huh. You're one of a kind, Run Ono-Marks. I never thought I'd see—It's Jozy. Jozy Jinx."

"Pleasure," I say, extending my hand. She takes it, starts running her fingers up and down my synth arm, making the haptics bristle.

"When this is all over, maybe we can celebrate at some clubs in the Overcity. I know places more interesting than GaGa's." She winks.

"Sure, Jozy. I think Navid would enjoy an old fashioned night on the town."

"Good. Well, now that we're on a first name basis, I was wondering if I could run a few more tests on your synth body?" Jozy asks. She stands up from the table and opens the sliding door. Jozy Jinx steps inside her loft, shimmer-hair goes platinum. She slinks over to the seating area, taps a screen on the holoprojector. Beside her, one of the couches slides, folds open, and flattens.

Stand up, stub my smoke, and follow her inside, holding what's left of my whiskey. "What kind of test're you planning on?"

Jozy Jinx unzips her bodysuit and lets it fall to the floor around her ankles. Naked as the day she was born, save for tattoos of circuits running up and wrapping around each leg from her knees to her hips, and another down her left arm to the wrist. She taps again at the holoprojector. New acid jazz combo disappears, and in their place a holo-fire roars, crackling. "I had to check your whole synth body when I brought you back online and did the recharge, so I would like to confirm my suspicions about its full functionality," she says. "You're not a bad kisser either, but what I'm most intrigued by is your combination of dexterity and an incredible aptitude for following instructions. Besides, consider this another demonstration of trust. How can we count on each other to be good friends and business partners if we can't be completely vulnerable?"

I finish the last of the whiskey. "You make a compelling argument. I should run one more stress diagnostic, just for good measure."

Walk toward her. She sits down on the edge of the bed, cocks her head, smiles. Shimmer-hair glows like a star. Almost blinding. She's angelic, skin luminous, eyes glinting. She reaches for the screen on the holoprojector, lowers the lights. Daylight fades to artificial darkness, floods with warm waves of neon pink. Circuit tattoo shimmers now, pulses of light coursing up and down the inked lines, flickering at the nodes. Sit down beside her, take off my jacket. Fingers trace the circuits on her thighs. Synth heart ramps up. She kisses me, takes my hand and places it on her breast. Holo-fire pops and rumbles.

six

Jozy sends a list of new hires to the screen in my Kento, waiting for me in her tower's garage. Secure channel, just her and me. Five candidates for the shady technobugger. None of them intimidating. Three interns, two from Overcity universities, sweater wearing readers, one older, former drone tech looking to "get in and change the system," seems most likely. Remaining two are longtime Bouq employees who work as liaisons to the Commonwealth Legislature in the Overcity. Jozy's good. Records on each are deep and dense.

One of the college kids, name Macy Lane, was left at an Undercity sanitation mech center, wrapped in solarsheeting, with no other info. Mechs protocol on living waste required immediate reporting to HomeCom Health. Corps pick up this baby, bring it to full health and put it on the adoption market in the Overcity. Bids went crazy, over ten figures because the newsfeeds ran the story nonstop. "A miracle child has survived desperate abandonment in the Undercity. Corporate heroes are ensuring her health and happiness and will promote her adoption with an as yet unheard of fundraising auction. HomeCom has generously pledged to invest 40% of proceeds toward developing life scanners for undeveloped areas of the Undercity. 'We want to ensure that something like this never happens again. Our life scanners will immediately recognize abandoned children allowing HomeCom to quickly pick up and offer them for adoption!' The remaining funds from the auction will be used for research and development essential to HomeCom's continued station in the Commonwealth." Kid got bought by a good family, celebrity faded some, managed to work academic and city connections to get in good with the Bouquet, do some charitable outreach to the Noncons, including serving as Commonwealth Ambassador to the Wastes.

None of the rest are so remarkable. Just stories you've heard before. Rich kid with a conscience. Political legacies hoping to one up their forebears. Tech who grew tired of working without purpose, wants to do something meaningful. Real question is which one is desperate and why. Don't start fooling around with a major political machine unless you need and expect something big in return.

Close the dossier file, ping coming in from Jozy, answer it. "Run," she says on screen. "I don't imagine this will be too tough a job for you, given your proven physical aptitude." She winks as if I wouldn't get it. "Just like before, I'll have eyes on you. Take out the leak, then come back here for another comprehensive performance assessment. I know you can do it, and if you don't I know I'll find someone who will." Another wink.

I nod. "Already feeling good about one lead. I'll be in touch."

"Drone tech?" she asks.

"Yeah. Obvious enough that it's either gotta be him or gotta not be him," I say. "Only one way to find out."

Rev up the Kento, Navid Francis's Kento, and throw it into the reverse. Give a little salute to Jozy on screen, "Save me a drink." She smiles, nods. Shimmer-hair glows platinum. She's got a tell. Deactivate the comm, tap the address of the drone tech, pull out of the tower's garage, passing top shelf autos on every level. Shit like these makes the Kento look quaint. On street level, I cruise through Avalon, Jozy's neck of the Over. Quiet day up here, clouds hanging over the field cast shadows, make the holos pop. Scant peds all illuminated, wearing solar-input sportswear. Irritating to look at, seems likelier to make them a target of a pissed off driver than to dissuade them. A couple LyfTek Haulers start setting up a stage on the sidewalk, butting up on a patch of greenspace. Must be continuing Recognition Day festivities. Folks in the Over tend to celebrate it for more than the day of. Must be nice to feel like saviors at your leisure.

Catch the Loop right outside Avalon. Screen points me straight to the drone tech's place, a decent condo complex in the Second. Know the place, started as a Cap tenement project. After they finished construction, it was too nice to "give away" so they sold to HomeCom. They found a way to make their investment worthwhile, of course. Looks like an open-floor studio, about a quarter the size of Jozy's, no terrace, just one way in and out. And based on the work schedule Jozy hacked, the guy's going to be home alone, watching Slashball matches or diddling himself. Catch him trying to clean himself, all the better. Intimidation's so much easier when the target's especially off guard. Watch for the Loop exit for the Second, punch it, slide the Kento across three lanes, down two, and slip down onto the Undercity streets.

Screen lights up. "Please standby for a message from the Commonwealth Undercity Second District." I forgot about this. Some zecs have been trying to make the Second happen for a few years. Part of the plan is to give it an "Overcity Feel" through welcome videos, event calendars, beautification projects that tend to only beautify the cash-positive parts, and ads. Actor-faced zec duo, one pretty, one rugged pop on screen. Wish there was a way to skip these. "Welcome to the Undercity's Second District, the premier up-and-coming entertainment locale for all Commonwealth citizens," one says. "We pride ourselves on inclusivity here. That's why everyone is welcome in the Second District," says the other. "Let's take a moment to offer a brief overview of the beautiful amenities in the Undercity's Not-So-Hidden Gem," says the first. "The Second is home to folks of all walks, human, synth-adaptive, full-synth, gay, straight, trans, clean, addict, cash-rich and cash-poor. Because of this beautiful mix, there are businesses to meet the needs of just about anyone who visits our district, no matter where they come from." "And that's not all, the Second offers melting pot housing opportunities unlike any other part of the Commonwealth." Actor-faced zecs laugh. "That's right. This is a place where you can really get to know your neighbors and get to know broad swaths of humanity, all at the same time!" "When the prompt appears on your screen, we encourage you to engage with our visitor's center application to help you make your stay in the Second one-of-a-kind." Both speak at once, "Enjoy your visit! We're happy to have you here!" Screen goes to black. Then text appears: **Paid for by the Second District Community Organization with a grant from the Bouquet Melting Pot Foundation.** Then the screen offers that visitor's center app. I don't bother.

Pull up outside HomeCom Regency Arms. Fancy name for a cash scheme. Lots of folks sitting on stoops, couple rooting through trash processors. Group of punks loitering, ogling folks as they go past, catcalling. Music blaring from some units in the building, three or four different genres, best I can tell. Hard to pick out. Some kids running around blasting each other with lightguns, giggling. Average day in an average place with above average branding. Plenty of parking, so I leave the Kento at the curb. Check my thigh compartment, pistol still there. Missed having it. Just didn't feel right without. Seems like the last twenty-four could've been a dream. Climb out of the car, lower the gullwing, activate the security, level four. Worst case a couple kids get zapped trying to finger the paint job. Next stop, the residence of R. James Leopold, drone tech.

Building doesn't have any holistic security, just an above door camera, and a quick flick of my hood takes care of that. Won't be reason to check the tapes anyway, ain't here to kill the guy, just to remind him of the boundaries of his ethics. Interior's laid out like any tenement, slightly improved. Halls are about half a meter wider than in my tower, doors are wider, taller. Must've been a spec error, or a drone programming issue. Something to ask the leak for small talk. Usually helps grease the wheels a bit, some friendly, inquisitive banter. Especially disarming if he's wanking it when I pop in. Jozy's data points me to the eighth floor, unit 895. Navigate the labyrinthine halls to a maglift bay at the tower's core. Older folks poke their heads out, stand talking to each other across the hall. Some kids are running around here too, lightguns again. Hall smells of cooking, sounds of music and screen noise. One argument. A couple instances of sensual engagement. Ride the lift up toward eight. On three a couple of party kids hop on, tripped and vaping, dressed for a dayclub, one with shimmer-face active. Enhancing the trip. They start giggling, get off at five to turn around. Old woman gets on at seven with a hovercart full of laundry, looks at me with immediate disdain, watches me like a hawk as I slide past the cart to get off on R. James Leopold's floor.

The eighth floor, like the others, is a labyrinth mixed with a cell block. Weave from the open doors of the lift, find the resident screen, take note of a few names, then tap on Leopold's, follow the light strip in the floor to his door. Funny how tech to improve delivery experience also improves investigatory experience. Unit 895's door looks like all of them, grey, numbered, inset camera. Wait out of the cam's view and activate my incog to HomeCom maintenance worker. Digitized jumpsuit loads all around me, orange and navy with the HC logo on the chest and back. Bite my lip and then muster the most important costume of all: the corporate smile. Grinning like you're getting paid. Approach the door, tap the buzzer under the cam. Hear a faint ping-pong echo behind the door. Wait for footsteps, a splash of shadow beneath the door. There it is. Smile, Run. Smile.

"Who's there?"

"HomeCom maintenance team," I say. "We've had reports of toxin filter issues on this floor. Can I come inside to run a few quick diagnostics?"

Pause. Shuffling feet. Might be putting on pants. Grabbing a weapon.

"I'm not having any problems in my unit," the voice says. "Uh, are you sure you're on the right floor?"

Smile while you talk. "I just checked Mrs. Anatoli's unit and there were traces, not the worst I've seen for sure." Laugh. "But I replaced her toxin filters to be safe. Same thing with the Cartwright residence. It sure would be great if I could just check out your system and make any necessary adjustments. HomeCom wants every day of your life to feel like... Home."

"Anatoli's and Cartwright's, huh?" the voice says. "Fine. Shit. Just a second."

Another pause. More shuffling feet, rustling. Might've been nude, jacking. Jozy's intel was strong. Minute passes. See the green light illuminate under the cam. Door slides open. Man matches the images from Jozy. It's him. R. James Leopold's a breathless man. Definitely mid-jack. Slicks his hair back, does one of those sweeping arm gestures to invite me inside.

"Sorry about the mess," R. James Leopold says. Booze caps, delivery bucket and pouches scattered everywhere. Screen on the wall tuned to some nature channel. Place is spare, just a couch, couple of book shelves, round bed in the corner, a couple drones on the floor in the back.

"Not at all, sir," I say. "It's HomeCom who's sorry for bothering you today. If you'll just point me toward your toxin filter, I'll take a look and get out of your hair."

R. James Leopold leads me to the maintenance column beside the open kitchen, taps on it like he's a real hands-on kind of guy. "Here you go. I haven't noticed any issues breathing or anything, so hopefully this won't cost me a lot."

Smile. Laugh. "Oh, Mr. Leopold, this service is complimentary. HomeCom cares about all of our residents and customers, and we strive to exceed a one hundred percent satisfaction guarantee."

Leopold chuckles. "I've got other complaints if you're here to guarantee satisfaction."

Smile big. "I'd be happy to take a quick holorecording with you after I'm done with the maintenance tasks. I can submit it to my superiors," I say. "For now, give me five or ten minutes to evaluate your toxin filter and I'll be back with you."

"Sure." R. James Leopold turns and walks back over to the couch, plops down, starts to scroll for content on the screen.

Pop open the toxin filter cover. Make some essential tapping, banging, and rattling sounds. Pull the filter, check it out. Blow on it. Fuck if I know how you maintain toxin filters. Probably should've had some kind of tool bag. Lucky that R. James Leopold isn't the attentive type. Kill a couple minutes rooting around in the column. Pull a card, shake a filter, tap on some shit. Most importantly, let my synth finger hack the in-unit emergency grid connection, set up a temp aural disrupt signal. Don't need any outside trouble showing up mid-conversation. Disengage the incog. HomeCom getup gone. Pop the thigh compartment, grip the pistol, and step on out of the maintenance column.

R. James Leopold doesn't look over as I approach. Engrossed in the screen. Flipping endlessly through newsfeeds, programs.

"Got that filter taken care of," I say, holding my iron at forehead height. "Seems like your system is just fine. I do have a couple of questions for you and I'll be on my way."

"I told you it wasn't a proble—" Leopold looks up, spies the barrel at his noggin, twists his face up real ugly. "What the fuck, man! Don't kill me. Please don't kill me! EMERGENCY! EMERGENCY! Why isn't it working?"

"It's disabled," I say. "It'll reactivate in a couple of hours. We need to have a conversation."

Leopold's shaking. "What... what about? I didn't do anything."

I smile. "No one ever did anything when there's a gun to their head," I say. "You've been working for the Bouqs. Been messing with their data, their hackkeys."

R. James Leopold frowns, tears form on his eyes. "I don't know what you're talking about. I... I've been working for the Bouqs, sure, but I didn't do anything with their data."

Press the barrel to his temple, increase the energy flow ratio. Makes a good noise, intimidating, just for show. Leopold squirms, starts sweating. "You expect me to believe someone with your talents for engineering isn't the guy responsible for engineering-heavy espionage?" Dial up the flow once more. More squirming. Rest my off hand on his shoulder. Synth reads his heart rate. Elevated. Let's see if he's lying. "I think you're playing the Bouqs for fools, trying to take them down from the inside. That's what it is, isn't it?"

"No. No! I set up some drones, okay?" he says. "That's it. I didn't do anything with a hackkey! I don't even know what you're talking about with the hackkey."

Reading comes through clear. No indicative spikes. Probably telling the truth. "What kind of drones?"

Leopold gulps. "Minis. Spying on the women's restroom and locker room. There's… a lot of hot young things working with the Bouqs and folks'll pay well for footage of them."

Goddamnit. Not the leaker. Just a grosso. Keep the gun on him, reach for a smoke, light it. "So that's your game? Selling ladies' privacy to whatever digital dickboi wants a wank?"

Leopold nods, eyes closed, face drenched. "I was going to quit in a few weeks. Just wanted to make a little extra money, and these guys would never get near any of the girls, see. It's not like I'm selling them out."

"Interesting perspective." I lower the pistol. "You're a real piece of shit, R. James Leopold. I'd report you to HomeCom for illegal content creation and techterrorism, but I think I've got something better for you." Dial the energy back sixty-five percent on the gun. Aim at his crotch. Fire. Blast of light exits the barrel, splashes Leopold right where it dangles.

Leopold screams, folds over, grabs at himself. "What the fuck, man!? What the fuck, man!"

Take a drag, exhale. "You'll be fine. You got three days until the stun wears off. Your dick'll be numb until then. Won't feel a thing, including if you're pissing yourself until your pants get warm. Recommend you alter your vocational path choice."

Leopold's got his hand in his pants, making sure everything's still there. It is. Looks up at me, teary-eyed, sweaty-faced, blubbering. "I'll report you! You won't get away with this."

Take another drag, tap my arm screen. Play the recording back.

"Minis. Spying on the women's restroom and locker room. There's... a lot of hot young things working with the Bouqs and folks'll pay well for footage of them."

"No. You won't," I say. "And unless you help me figure out who is causing trouble for the Bouqs, I'm going to turn three days into fourteen." Dialing up the energy five percent.

R. James Leopold squirms some more. Eyes down, shaking his head. "That girl. The one from the newsfeed. She was on one of the videos, complaining about how the Commonwealth is all bullshit, made her into a stunt. She said something about taking revenge."

"Convenient memory."

"She said it right before she took her top off in the locker room," he says. "I watched that section a few times when I was editing the final product. Customers don't want them talking. Much less about politics. It ruins the mood."

"Show me the footage. I know you're the type to keep the raw stuff on file."

R. James Leopold nods. "I'll have to pull it up on the screen. Don't shoot me, okay?"

I gesture with the pistol. Leopold stands up, fiddles with his junk again, waddles over to the screen on the wall. Makes some taps, retinal scanner reads him, opens a private file. Video plays. He wasn't lying. Macy Lane, miracle child of the Undercity's right there, talking to someone on her device, tearing the Commonwealth, the Bouqs, the Caps a new one. "They never gave a solitary fuck about me. They paraded me around like a museum piece. Used me for photo ops. Turned my suffering into a feel good story they could sell everyone and left me to raise myself and sort out all their shitty rules and regs. I didn't want to be the poster child for these clowns and now that's all I'll ever be!" Definitely the words of someone jilted by the system with a motive for revenge. Audiofeed gets garbled, and then Macy Lane starts undressing.

"Shut it down," I say. "I've got what I need."

"You're sure you don't want a look?" R. James Leopold asks, eyebrows raised.

"You sure you want to keep your dick?" Dial up the energy. The digital squeal really lets you hear the kind of pain you'll feel.

Leopold flinches. Shuts the video down. "I told you. What'd I tell you?"

"Yep. You managed a semi-good deed," I say. "Good for you. Now, you're going to erase that and all the other footage, or I'm going to erase it for you."

"But, the cash."

"Easy come, easy go, pal," I say. "You'll find other ways to put cash together. We all do."

R. James Leopold deletes every drone footage file on the system, lets me take a gander at the records to verify, just about breaks down in tears.

"I don't want to come back here," I say. "And I don't think you want me to come back either."

He shakes his head.

"Good." Reactivate the incog, looking fully HomeCom again. Holster the pistol. Give him a smile. "You have a nice day now. HomeCom cares."

seven

Jozy's info sends me back to the Over. "Macy Lane's living alone in Tian," she says. "Too bad Leopold wasn't the leaker, but I'm happy you made him uncomfortable. Probably the longest he'll ever last is with that stunned dick."

"Good one," I say.

"I know. I'm very funny," Jozy replies. "Now, just take the Loop back up and Tian is two neighborhoods north of—"

"I know where Tian is. Grew up in Elysium, remember?"

III

She shoots me a dirty look. "You're awfully torqued. Someone's battery getting low? Need a charge?"

Check the meter. 82%. "I'm fine. Just don't like wasting time."

"You took care of Leopold, Run," Jozy says. "That's a good thing."

"Sure. I could spend the rest of my life taking down technopervs in the Commonwealth, and I'd be bailing water from a sinking ship with a holobucket."

"Fine, be negative," she smirks. "Getting into the Princess Towers isn't going to be like an apartment building in the Second. I'm transmitting a temp override employment ID. Navid Francis is going to be a representative from Macy Lane's alma mater, Commonwealth EduUniFac. Already messaged her that the school wants to recognize her for her work to improve the city through political progress. This'll be a meeting to discuss the details of her appearance on campus and on promotional materials for the school, so wear a suit and try to sound professional until you get inside."

"I've got just the incog." Flick it on to give Jozy a glimpse.

"Looking good, Run. Go take care of this leaker kid and I'll be waiting for you with a charge table and some eager... circuits. I've got some new ideas, been playing with some rough schematics, and I want to try a few new diagnostics on your root system." She hits 'root system' hard. Winks. "But, that assumes you survive, to see if you survive my... tests. We're going total silence from here. Don't be stupid and try to ping me. We don't want any Overcity signal enthusiasts picking us up on accident. As always I will be watching. Don't get yourself killed."

"When's this watching going to result in doing anything to help?" I say, trying to lighten up.

"As soon as I'm tired of seeing you work, synthboi."

Jozy cuts the comm. Synthboi? Not sure I like that.

Pull the Kento into Tian. District's mostly like any other in the Over, towers, park space, clubs, shit like that. Tian's special because of its tiered Wild Space. Commonwealth built a huge outdoor nature preserve, two-hundred stories tall, all connected with natural-looking inclines and fake rivers and tributaries. Never seen it in person. Built after I moved down. Sight to behold, even driving underneath. Between four LyfTek Princess Towers, layer after layer of suspended countryside, woods, jungle, mountains. At the top, a great peak, frosted with snow that falls via LyfTek ClimaTek. Stories say there are polar bears, lynx, penguins, other extinct animals up there. Clones of course. Can't manage to make more the old fashioned way. Must be weird, seeing your genetic duplicate searching for food. Wonder if they can tell. Whole Wild Space is that way. Forests filled with dead and gone animals, insects. Countryside and jungle too. LyfTek boasts the most elegant synthesized nature experience this side of the Last Crisis. Charge a bundle to go inside too. Mostly because the animals are wild as they can be. Ten or fifteen Overcitiers get lost in the Wild Space each year, eaten alive or eaten dead. Never been myself because there's plenty of opportunity to get fucked out here. Not going to throw precious cash at the chance to have the thirty-second iteration of Phil the Boxing Kangaroo beat my ass.

Macy Lane's in the fourth Princess Tower. The one most covered in holos, subsidized housing is what the Overcity calls it. Looks like a monument to HomeCom,

LyfTek, PalCorp, OppTech, Rambler, Transit, Kento, CommonCash, PerpetMot, the Cap, the Bouquet, Denco and others. Holos run together on their revolutions around the tower, makes a real mess, but the corps know folks are looking. Especially folks who live in the tower, get a view of whatever ad comes rolling by. Never can just get a little help. Always a tradeoff.

Tower has a valet. Activate the incog and get suited and booted as I pull up. Navid Francis, Commonwealth EduUniFac administrator, slips under the rising gullwing on his Kento, taps temp keycred to the valet, and watches the car zip out of sight toward the Princess Towers parking column. Better not catch them joyriding. Pass through the massive glass double doors, holos bouncing all around them, into the lobby. Even the subsidized Princess Tower has the trademark lobby. Cavernous city block with polished obsidian floors, color-shifting synthcrystal columns running up three stories with a balcony mezzanine of shops, clubs, and restos circling overhead. Aural tech silences any echo, and diffuses conversation. All you hear is the gentle tinkle of Nouveau Classique Digital flowing from a robo-grand in the middle of the room by some seating. Reception desk is front and center, similarly obsidian, with three attractive workers in ornament-covered Princess Tower uniforms behind it. All three smile as the glass doors slide shut behind me.

"Welcome to Princess Tower Four," one says. "Would you like assistance in finding your destination today?"

"If you don't know your destination, we have an all Towers tour starting in thirty minutes," another says.

"Or perhaps you're here for the Wild Space," says the third. "Tour packages and survivalist adventures are available for reasonable cash."

"Here to see Macy Lane," I say. "She's on the twenty-sixth floor, I think."

One of the attractive receptionists looks down at a screen. "Yes. Miss Lane is on the 26th floor. Is she expecting you, mister—?"

"Francis, Navid Francis. I'm with Commonwealth EduUniFac."

The second worker looks up at me and beams. "I see here that you're an esteemed guest of our most esteemed guest. Does this mean that Undercity Macy is going to be sharing her story of survival with your students?"

"She's such a miracle," says the third.

Smile. "I'm not at liberty to share the nature of our visit, but rest assured, Miss Lane will be recognized by Commonwealth EduUniFac for her contributions to this city."

Two of the receptionists gasp. The other asks, "This will be on the newsfeed, right? I don't want to miss it."

Nod. "I have some connections, so yes, I am sure there'll be a story about Macy Lane on the newsfeed soon. Is she ready to see me?"

First receptionist looks back at their screen, looks up. Nods. "She is. Please take maglift number 5 at the rear of the lobby. It's been assigned to deliver you, Mr. Francis."

"Thank you. You've all been very helpful," I say.

"Thank you for visiting Princess Tower Four. Please give our regards to Miss Lane."

"I shall," I say, giving as debonair a salute I can muster before strolling, casually but purposefully toward the maglifts. One of them says, "I almost went to Commonwealth EduUniFac," as the others giggle. Over can be a silly place.

Maglift takes me direct to Macy Lane's unit. Her adoptive parents must've left it to her, or the Commonwealth did something good and didn't overpublicize it for once. Place occupies a quarter of the floor, has a holofountain, holoart covering each wall, sequenced to display—at least today—an array of classic paintings, Da Vinci, Monet, Picasso. That sort of stuff. Macy Lane sits at a massive screen terminal, portions showing entertainment content, others strings of processing code. Turns in a swivel chair to face me. Head shaved, nose pierced, chain runs from there to her ear. "You with the school? Sit down over there. Be done in a sec."

Oblige her, walk over to the seating, sit professionally, manneredly. Macy Lane's fingers fly all over the screens before her. Like a trance. Looks like she's got eight arms at times. Can't tell what she's doing, but no sense getting defensive now. Princess Tower isn't the place you want to be firing pistols. Navid Francis isn't the pistol-firing type either. Busy myself looking at the art on the wall. Classic stuff mutates the longer you look at it. Unsettling but slick. Have to remember to ask where she got the tech, install it at home when I'm debt free.

Macy Lane finally finishes whatever she's doing, walks over, sits across from me. "So what does EUF want?"

Clear my throat. Smile. "Well, Miss Lane, Commonwealth EduUniFac would like to invite you to return to campus so that we might recognize you for your contributions to the city, and the folks beyond its walls," I say. "We've heard that you've been working with the Bouquet of late, and that combined with the goodwill tour you did with the Cap in your youth, shows us that you're uniquely dedicated to this community."

Macy Lane pulls a device from her pants pocket, starts staring at it, tapping the screen. I wait. "So, what's in it for me? Cash or honorary diplomas or fuckall like that?" She goes back to looking at the device.

"There's no prize, to speak of, Miss Lane, but—"

"Not interested," she says. "You can leave." She stands up and walks toward the terminal, still plugging at the device in her hands.

"Miss Lane," I say. "EUF hopes only to continue your leadership position in the community, the one you were born into."

Macy Lane scoffs, starts laughing real big. "Leadership position? Really? Like I'd want to lead this shithole and its empty, showy, selfish citizens. This place is a joke, and I bet you know it. Makes it even more insulting that you'd try this game in the first place."

Fuck. "I know that the Commonwealth isn't perfect, Miss Lane. Nor is EUF. But I assure you this is no game. We genuinely want to honor your wo—"

She points the device in her hand at me. Shit. Incog crashes immediately. Navid Francis's suit disappears. Just little old me on display. Check my forearm, non-essential systems are locked. Can't open the thigh compartment. Can't go incog. Can't run diagnostics. Can't move my legs, can't stand. Stuck sitting here on her couch. Macy Lane made me. Shit.

"Don't worry, dummy," she says. "I'm not going to hurt you. But you're going to tell me why you're here right the fuck now. You one of these obsessives? Been looking for Miracle Macy to save you from yourself, absolve you for fucking around on your partner, tell you all about the dirty details of being abandoned as an infant?"

If Jozy's watching, now would be a great time to do something with what she's seeing. "I'm not from EUF, you're right. I'm just a hired hand. A contractor. I was asked to get some background on you and your connection to the... Noncons. Buyers are interested in using your inroads."

"Someone wants to fuck with the Noncons?" she says.

Shake my head. "I don't know what they want with them. Just wanted me to contact you as a 'trusted person'."

"And they had you dress up EUF? Idiots. It's the Cap or the Bouqs, or both. Must be." She stares at me, looking for a tell. I don't give her one. "Tell me who you're working for and I'll reactivate your non-essentials, lickety split."

"I can't divulge that information," I say. "They'll kill me if I do." Buy it.

"Convenient arrangement," she says. "Look. I don't care who it is. They're all crooked, from corps to gov. Nothing but cash-grabbing shadowboxers. You shouldn't be working for any of them, unless you're working through them."

"I take whatever jobs come my way," I say. "Cash reigns." Finally, a little honesty.

Macy Lane laughs. "Sure. Problem is, they own you. They already own everybody, know it or not." She keeps working the device in her hand. "I'm not telling you shit about the Noncons, but I'll give you a little gift before I kick your ass out of here." She taps at the holofountain, and pulls one of the screens from the terminal into it. File root system appears, looks like a list of recordings, categorized by corps and gov parties, dated. Macy Lane pulls open a Bouquet file, dated three days ago, opens it. My photo comes up. My real name comes up. Fuck. "See, this is you, Run Ono-Marks. You're working with the Bouquet as a contractor, and I'm guessing they want you to stop me from bugging and cracking their hackkeys and encoded message sys. What's funny, to me anyway, is that you don't know the half of it. How curious are you feeling?"

"I feel like you're going to show me no matter how I answer."

"Bingo bongo," she says. Brings up a video file. Bouquet headquarters, the real one up in the Over, Harriet Alpha standing before a committee of electeds and zecs. "As you can see, our covert incursion activities are showing signs of success in altering the Caps' and Noncons' attempts at establishing a trade relationship," Alpha says. "We've discussed the essential nature of maintaining the Bouquet narrative as a heartfelt savior and these actions keep us securely in that position." Alpha displays a map of the region, the city and the Wastes.

"Look here, by repeatedly hitting these supply checkpoints in Incog, we can keep the Cap believing that the Noncons are stealing from them, while keeping the Noncons believing that the Caps are attacking them and their autonomy. Our friends at LyfTek will continue to execute each mission, for a fee, detaching us from culpability. Then we swoop in for the good PR. Genius, really." Video file ends. Macy Lane shoots me a serious look. "Do you want to see more?"

I nod. "Bouqs are double crossing the Noncons and Caps by making it look like they're attacking one another," I say. "Honestly, makes sense. Easy to provide aid when you create the conflict."

"You're smarter than you look," Macy Lane says. Pulls up another video file. This time it's the Caps headquarters in the Over. Story's the same though. Caps and zecs discussing undermining the Bouqs and Noncons. "Clearly we must triple our efforts to establish corporate offices in the Wastes where we can fold in the Noncons," one zec says. "We've added subtle toxins to the water and food supplies sent outside the city, this should force the Noncons to return to

123

Commonwealth control. Soldiers will deal with any noncompliants. And by encoding each toxic shipment with Bouquet serial tags, it'll all look like more incompetence from the bleeding hearts." Another zec, behind a big desk, speaks, "This goes hand in hand with our hacks of Bouquet voting systems?" The other answers, "Of course. We will continue to undermine target citizens in the Undercity while blaming the Bouqs for doing nothing to stop us." "Good, the big zec says. "And the planned attack?" The other replies, "Yes. PalCorp's team will ensure that the Undercity remains as dangerous as necessary to keep the Bouquet in the minority."

That's what they were up to at that orphanage. Caps keeping their might-makes-right in place. "Look," I say. "If you're trying to prove to me that there's no good side, I already know."

Macy Lane grins. "The Bouqs and the Caps are killing us on purpose. They're killing Noncons on purpose. Just to stay in control. You should be mad."

"I am. Tale as old as time," I say. "Power is power."

Macy Lane pulls up another video file. Footage of the Wastes, Noncons. No sound. Noncons living in a city of their own out there. No tents or hovels. No kids kicking dust, looking weak and sick. A bona fide community. Folks dressed nice enough for the Over, growing plants outside, food. No masks, no breathers. Just folks living. In the Wastes. Video goes on for five minutes. Slow strolls up and down Noncon streets lined with older autos, retroed and rumbling. Shops, homes, a gov-looking building. They've built a life for themselves. Nothing like what shows on the newsfeed. Macy Lane lets the video play on a loop. Walks around it, through it, points at every remarkable structure and Noncon.

"Things aren't as they seem," she says. "They want us to believe there's no other way. They want us reliant on the Commonwealth, divided from the Noncons, divided by Overcity and Undercity. All just to keep power, Run Ono-Marks. All to keep power."

"Where'd you get this data?"

"A terminal here, a system hack there. Nothing's doctored if that's what you're getting at. Think of me as an oracle, providing you truth and guidance, an awakening," she says.

125

"Alright. Trust no one and nothing," I say. "Not much of a leap."

Macy Lane shrieks, real high pitched. "You don't understand! You aren't listening!" Brings up another video file. Jozy's on it. Talking with Harriet Alpha in that big office down in the Bouq bunker. "You understand what we're looking for then?" Alpha asks. Jozy Jinx nods. Goddamnit. I'm an idiot. Sucker for shimmer-hair and a hard charge. "We need a synth with nothing to lose. Should be easy enough to track." "Good," Alpha says. "Then we install an EMP and send them to the Caps to erase everything they have. The setback will allow the Bouquet to rise and lead the Commonwealth for good, and our corporate partners will ensure that nothing changes in the day-to-day." "Sure. Whatever," Jozy says. "Just transfer the cash and I'll get you a synth." Video ends.

"Having trouble putting it together?" Macy Lane asks.

"I'm the synth," I say. "They're gonna use me to blow up the Cap."

Macy Lane nods and smiles, gets right in my face. "That's right, Run. They played you. Whatever they promised you isn't coming. That EMP will turn you into a puddle. Along with the Cap data stores."

Bitter pill. Bitterer that Jozy's in on it. Makes sense though. Always knew how to pick them. When I first went synth, used to do small jobs with an Undercity rat named Ropio. Seemed like a good kid, did three or four jobs together, transporting goods, organs, whatever. One day, HomeCom security pulls us over. Ropio gives me up the sec they pull him from the Hauler in exchange for a lighter sentence. Lucky for me, the package wasn't stolen, just trying to avoid paying gate fees and taxes. Ten days I was back out. Never saw Ropio again. Stopped working with anyone, until Jozy. Should've replaced my brain with synth too, probably wouldn't be so stupid.

"What's in this for you?" I ask. "Want me to take down both the Bouqs and the Caps? Show the whole Commonwealth that their leaders and zecs are only out for themselves? Prove that the Noncons are the only hope anyone's got so folks flood out into the Wastes and ruin that shit too?"

Macy Lane laughs. Brings her face close to mine again. "Surprise, surprise. You're secretly a heroic type." She laughs louder. "I just wanted you to understand the depth of betrayal around you. From what I see here, you've got a 60% charge left, and as soon as I send a message, everyone will be looking for you, ready to take you out for what you know."

"So full-on sadism then?"

"They won't be looking for me, then, either. Now will they?"

Of course. Played by the player who's playing the players. How quaint. "Good deal. Let me go and I'll keep them busy while you keep getting revenge for being a media darling."

She points the device at me, taps. Fire courses through me. Can't double over for being frozen in place. Just incredible pain on pain on pain. Bite my lip and wince. Grunt.

"You're cute," she says, stopping the device. "I was abused, made a poster child of the fake veneer of goodness that everyone in this disgusting city hides behind while lining their pockets and poisoning anyone who gets in their way." Macy Lane paces, circling me on the couch. "I had considered setting you up as a bomb myself, sending you out to make chaos, pin it all on both of them. I've got enough synth parts to make you convincingly look like two bombers. But when I sent a couple encoded messages that I knew you were coming here, well, the bidding started high and went higher. So, I'll be giving you up for enough cash to leave the Commonwealth for Oceanside or Pine Cliffs... haven't decided yet. You know what they say, 'If you can't change the world, change yourself.'"

"No morals for the moralistic then?" I say.

She sends another fiery blaze through my body. I yell. Can't hold it in. Everything burns, neck to toes. "When in Rome, synthboi. Going to put you in standby now. I'm not stupid enough to let you wriggle your way out of this like you did at CommonCash." She points her device once more. Feel my heart slow, breaths shallow, body goes weak. Start slumping forward, eyes heavy, tired. Everything goes bl█████

^^^o

Must be dreaming. Canopy of tree branches, birds chirping, sound of rushing water, a breeze. Still can't move. Dawns on me. The Wild Space. Boreal forest. Middle of the stack, probably middle of the park. Perfect place for an exchange. Flickers of light stab the corners of my vision. Movement. Won't be lucky enough for it to be a bear or something else. Funny if Macy Lane's little plan ended with my head getting

129

bitten off. Interesting way to go at least. Not going to be that lucky.

"Looks like it's in good condition," one voice says.

"Yes. Worth the cash to get that cunt, Lane, out of our hair for good," another says.

"Pick it up and load it into the cart. The sooner we get it back to HQ the better."

Heavy bootsteps crunch in the dirt. Five, no, six sets. Group of PalCorp militia, clutching rifles, loom over me. Behind them a zec and a uniformed Cap. PalCorp stow their weapons, kneel down, grab my arms and legs. Try to fight. Can't move. Not a stitch. They lift me up, dump me in a hovercart. Too small, my legs fold up, knees at my chest. Good thing synth parts won't hurt tomorrow, if there's a tomorrow. Stare at them. Try to tell them to fuck off. Mouth not working yet.

"Doesn't look scary to me," PalCorp soldier says. "Standard gutterpunk from the Under."

"That is why you're PalCorp, lack of vision. Take it to the Hauler now," the uniformed Cap barks. "We will catch up with you."

Sky changes as they pull the hovercart out of the Wild Space. Canopy gives way to clear blue sky, clouds shaped like animals. See a wolf growling at the Sun.

Try to overhear the Cap and zec talking, best I can make out... "Bouqs won't know what him them." "And PalCorp security sales will skyro—" Voices lost to rolling water, wind rustling through tall trees.

eight

Rattle around in the back of a PalCorp Hauler for an hour, maybe two. Must've avoided the Loop entirely. All surface streets. Stays away from Hauler checkpoints. No questions mean no answers. Finally come to a stop, PalCorp soldiers climb in, pull the hovercart out of the Hauler. Not gentle, bump my head a few times. Laugh about it. They drag the cart up a ramp. Best I can see is a tower-filled sky loaded with holos and huge Commonwealth banners. Ambrosia. Must be. All the gov and corps have satellite offices here, in Republic Park. Cams above the door. Wait while they flash their creds. Door glows green. Cart passes through. Oafs at the handle bang it into the doorjamb on the way. "Watch it, dummy," one says. "You watch it! Synths don't feel. Who cares?"

Halls are narrow, cement and steel. No holos. No windows. Boots echo against the walls, tinny. Try to count the lights in the ceiling, get a sense of distance. Twenty-three lights, each about two meters long. Turn a corner, left, keep counting lights, forty more. Big place. Not surprising. Cap headquarters should be big, it's got to hold a lot of shitheads, zecs, corp guards, all the worst from outside condensed and concentrated.

"Rumor is they wanna use this synth to put the Bouqs to bed once and for all."

Guard laughs. "About time someone did. Disgusting Bouqs think taking care of folks matters!? How stupid can you be? Every man for himself. Survival of the fittest. Show me yours and I'll show you mine."

Like Cap catchphrases in a sonic mixer with a bot. Doubt the guard has any idea how much his bosses at PalCorp rely on gov support. Still can't talk, fortunately, so I don't have to hold my tongue.

"With the Bouqs out of the way, guys like us can finally get ours."

"Fuck right!"

Another couple turns, right twice this time. Fifteen and thirty-six lights. Deep in the belly now. Must be the center of the Cap. Exit what ends up being the final hallway, ceiling and walls open up into a massive atrium. Four stories, maybe five, tall glass top like a cathedral. Footsteps echo louder. Violin music wafts toward me, getting louder. Dead center of the vaulted ceiling is above. Cart stops suddenly, guard stomps the hoverbrake, jostling me onto my side.

"Be careful, you morons. Our esteemed guest does not deserve this shoddy treatment!"

"Sorry, boss," one of the guards mutters.

The Boss? Hank Millennia. Seven time leader of the Cap, five time President of the Commonwealth. Former pro fighter in the NeonCube. I knew I knew that voice.

"Synth looks fine to me," says the other.

Heavy footsteps, dress shoes, slap near. "If I wanted your assessment of the condition of Mr. Ono-Marks I'd have asked you for it. Wait outside. If I need even the remotest modicum of your limited capacity to help me, I will call for you."

Bootsteps trail away from the cart, fall silent behind the woosh of a sliding door. The boss steps closer, leans over the hovercart, hulking frame casting a broad shadow. Turn to look at him.

"Are you comfortable in there, Mr. Ono-Marks?" he says.

Can't really shake my head, but muster a turn of it to make contact.

"Ah, you still can't speak, of course. A pity. But, being the fan of efficiency that I am, this will expedite our conversation, and I'm certain you will want to hear what I have to offer," he says. "But first, I'll remove you from this conveyance." Millennia hoists me out of the cart, plops me in a chair on the powerless side of the desk. Walks around, sits down in a big wingback. Pulls a cigar from its cradle over an ashtube set into the glasstop. Chomps on it. "We haven't met, but you probably know me. Your president. Your warrior king. Your NeonCube champion. Your chief executive of PolyCo Amalgamated. Not to boast, but without me, there'd be nothing in the Overcity or the Undercity, no PalCorp, no FamilyTech, no HomeCom, no CommonCash, no LyfTek, no nothing. That's why you should feel very special today, Mr. Ono-Marks.

135

Because the man who controls the destinies of tens of millions is about to make you an offer."

Millennia puffs at the cigar, stands dramatically, blows rings, turns his back to me. Powerless, I sit. "You know, in the Cube I learned the most important lesson in life. Fight until you win. You follow me? Fight. Until. *You. Win.* Some folks might instead say, 'fight to win,' but that makes winning a goal rather than an outcome. Every night for eight years in the Cube I faced combatants who were fighting *to* win. How many of them did?" Millennia waits a beat, looks at me. "None. Why? I was fighting *until I won.* That's why I destroyed my opposition in the Cube and that's why I've destroyed my opposition in gov, whether they be zecs who think their success under my supervision is their own, or the Bouqs with their pathetic plans to rebrand this city as a place for everyone. Guess what? It's not for everyone. The Commonwealth is for winners. And what do winners do?" He looks at me again, expectantly. "They fight until they win. And no one in this disgusting, violent world is going to win if they think this city was built for them. They should be happy to have it built by them for their betters! Or they should be cowards like the Noncons and go hide in the desert until they fucking die." He walks out from behind the desk, makes a circle behind me, dress shoes slapping the floor. "You understand this, you must. You chose a synthetic body because you were fighting until you won. You may not have won yet, but you've lived in this city long enough to taste victory and stew in defeat. You know as well as I do that the Bouqs are soft, meaningless children of slogans. They won't do what must be done to survive. They'd rather coddle the Commonwealth and hope that folks rise up to change the world. That's why I want you to destroy them. I want you to extinguish their holos and eradicate their empty speeches. I want us to win together."

Better that I can't talk or move. Fidgeting around Hank Millennia, worse yawning, likely to leave me with a handful of my own teeth. I blink at him, trying to convey my comprehension.

"Of course, you want to know what's in it for you, don't you? You're not living for others like some pussweasel. You're out for yourself. One person can make a difference, but that one person had better be well compensated. Good. I like that about you. Sign of a real champion," Hank Millennia says. "In exchange for wiping the Bouq secret headquarters, and mercing anyone who's foolish enough to try to stop you, I am willing to make you an official Officer of Freedom in the Cap. That's right. You'd be just the third Officer of Freedom in the Commonwealth, along with my dear, departed brother, killed by the Noncons in the Second Separation, and myself the first and truest Officer of Freedom this place has ever known. As such, you'll get a three-floor penthouse in Princess Tower One, full service, you want dayclub boys and girls they'll be there, you want to punch some Undercity scumbag in the mouth we'll deliver. Only thing you won't be able to order any day, any time is me. You'll live on Commonwealth credit, no more cash, no more debt. And, the pièce de résistance, a synth body that will never run out of juice, never die. You could spend a whole month fucking the brains out of a horde of hot young things and not only would never break a sweat, you'd never need a breather. That's power, Mr. Ono-Marks. Power I am offering to you. And all I ask in return is that you meet up with your friends in the Bouquet and ruin them, as gruesomely as you want..."

He sits back down at the desk, ashes the cigar, puffs again, and leans back in his chair, kicking his feet up on the clear desktop. "I wish you could speak, Mr. Ono-Marks. I imagine your head is swimming with questions. Let me answer one for you as I'm sure you'd ask it: Once the Bouquet is dead, the Cap can stop wasting time undermining their silly words and ideas. We can stop applying resources to elections and start applying them to rewarding the winners in our Commonwealth. You will be one of those winners, rewarded for your dedication and your spirit."

Millennia brings up a holo titled: My Vision. Everyone's got a presentation these days.

"You see, when the Cap no longer faces opposition, petty as they are, we can complete our plans for this city," he continues. "We can clean up the scourge of the Undercity, wipe the debris there off the map, turn it into a glorious reeducation camp dedicated to redeeming those who are able, and wrenching whatever value we can out of those who are not. There won't be a Bouq or Bouq sympathizer left. Learn or die. The Cap fights until it wins. And atop it all, you, Mr. Ono-Marks. They will look up to you. They will fear you. They will worship you. And you'll never have to deign to speak with them because you will be a true winner, almost as much as I."

A chime sounds from a screen on Hank Millennia's desk. He looks down at it, then back at me, grins, cigar perched between his large teeth. "A notification from

139

Miss Lane. Seems that you should be capable of answering my offer in three... two... one..."

Feel a surge of energy course through me, voice buzzes in my head, Macy Lane, recorded, says, "Time's up." Feet, legs, torso, arms, neck, heart starts beating normal, lungs filling fully, everything's back online. Quick diagnostic comes back with all checks. Charge at 45%. Lane put a timer on whatever that device did. Hope it can't be reactivated. Last thing I need is life as a marionette. More so than it is already.

"Please take a moment to reacquaint yourself with self-control, Mr. Ono-Marks," Millennia says. "After that, you can shower me with your joy at my generous offer."

"Don't need a moment," I say, mouth dry. "You're giving me an even better deal than the Bouqs tried. I could live forever in the total comfort of the Over. Only consequence is whatever comes of you taking full control of the Commonwealth."

Millennia puffs his cigar. "Well said. And, obviously, you wouldn't experience those consequences unless you tried standing against me." He clenches his fist. "And that would be foolish."

"I've seen the Cube. You were a behemoth. Broke the Kinzie Triplets in two rounds," I say. "You got another one of those?" Point to his cigar.

Hank Millennia beams. "I have *all the cigars*. And you will too." Pulls a drawer out in the desk, takes a cigar, clips it, hands it to me. "Light?"

Shake my head, flick open the thumb on my left hand, pop a flame. "I got my own." Puff.

"Resourceful," Millennia says. "That's how I beat the Kinzie's you know. Might and mind. Mind and might."

"Cube wall drop cutting Buck Kinzie in half didn't hurt."

"Nothing hurts when you win," Millennia says. "If my timing weren't perfect, I'd've lost an arm. Didn't lose it. Buck lost everything."

Smile. "Sure did. Brothers too. Honestly, a massacre."

He ashes his cigar. "They knew what they signed up for."

"And the strongest came out on top," I say.

He points at me. "Exactly. I'm glad we're of similar minds."

Ash my cigar, puff. "Oh, we're not," I say. "I think you're a madman, and your plan is going to mean

141

millions of good folks locked up to die, all so you and some zecs can grab a little more cash. Be nice to live forever, lots of reasons, but don't think I can do it knowing all those people would suffer. Not at that price, anyway."

Hank Millennia laughs. "This is not a negotiation."

"I think it is," I say. "See, I've got access with the Bouqs, and they definitely know I'm here by now. I don't have to have a side to know that I'm worth something to both."

Millennia walks around from behind the desk, grabs me by the jacket lapels, lifts me straight out of my chair. Strong fucker. NeonCube tells no lies. Don't struggle. Just breathe slowly, slip the thigh compartment open. Slow. Real slow.

"You have your choice in this endless conflict," he says. "Our directness against their niceties. The results are the same. Look at the Commonwealth as it is! So much waste. So much violence. So much fear. I can make our citizens proud of this place, and all we have to do is extinguish the Bouquet and their attachment to words that clog the conversation, pollute minds, and allude to a world even they don't want... because they'd become obsolete."

"I'm thinking about opting out," I say. Reach down, grab the iron from my thigh compartment, raise it, pull the trigger. Hank Millennia sees me coming, throws me across the room. Slide along the floor, slump against the wall, pistol spins away. Brute comes charging, lowers his head, bull rushes me. Shoulder straight to the gut, pins me to the wall, starts throwing hands, whaling on my face fast enough to keep me lifted. Bad idea. Should've taken the deal. Pop the blades in my hands, take a stab, catch some meat. Millennia grunts, grins. Misses getting bloody, looks turned on by it. Grabs me by the throat, flings me again. Slide into the desk, try to grab the iron on the way passed, can't get it. Charge meter blinks 50%. Plenty left if I survive. Climb to my feet, get in stance. Millennia comes charging again. Duck and dive, throw elbows in his back, sweep his leg. He's built like a tree, leg bounces right off. Try another kick. Throw an uppercut and catch his chin, rake with the blades, draw a little blood. Doesn't slow him down. Eyes black like a ope-head. Millennia reaches down, grabs my face in his meaty paw, puckering.

"Opting out of being a champion means choosing death, Mr. Ono-Marks," he says. "You've made your choice. Goodbye." Starts squeezing. Jaw aches. Hear

143

bone buckle. Kick out a blade from my foot, throw my best roundhouse, catch him in the calf. Millennia buckles, falls to a knee, drops me. Sprint toward my gun, dive, grab it, aim at the big boss.

"I'm not afraid of your toy," he says.

"No guns in the NeonCube." Fire a warning shot across his shoulder, graze him, hot meat and gunpowder smell hits the air. Millennia grunts, grits his teeth, spits. "I won't miss next time," I say.

"You won't have a chance," he says. Millennia slaps the screen on his desk, alarm sounds loud. "You'll be full of holes in a moment." Starts laughing. Mad man.

Footfalls in the distance. Boots. PalCorp coming. Lower the pistol, turn to run for the door. Millennia taps his screen again. Laughs louder. Ten or twelve militia burst in, rifles up, me in their sights. "Stand down, assailant," one says. "You are hereby under arrest for the attempted assassination of the President of the Commonwealth."

"Shoot him, idiots," Hank Millennia says. "Kill him."

Pause is enough to get a drop. Slide in, leg up, stab the lead PalCorp in the leg, flip over, slice the throat of another with my hand. Body blows, bloody ones, to a third. Three down. Dive, jump kick, flip. Throw haymakers. Grab a drop rifle, fire wild, catch another four. Spin and aim. Millennia charging in again, hits me square, knocks the gun out of my hand, grabs me by the leg. Dangling. Fuck. This is it. At least I got a good time out of it. Rifle barrels all over me, bloody faces seething, now they want me to die, not just a job anymore. Millennia hefts me up, grins, laughs, teeth gritted and shining. "Do it," he says.

Wait for rifle shots to ring out. Instead, glass shattering. Above, twenty masked black-clads come rolling down on ropes from the roof, firing all the way. One, two, four, six PalCorps drop wounded. Millennia yells, throws me down, synth back takes the impact. I crumple. From the floor, I see the mercs pick off the remaining security, five of them hold guns on Millennia.

"We don't want to kill you, sir. We just want the asset."

"That's why you're weak," Hank Millennia says.

Lead merc powers up his rifle, nods and the others follow suit. Gentle hum of a vaporizing amount of energy loading up. "Just because we don't want to doesn't mean we won't. There won't be anything left of you but a pile of ash."

145

Millennia comprehends the situation. Bites his lip. "Take him. I can destroy him, and each of you, later."

"We're sure you will, sir," lead merc says. "Move, team. Time to go."

Mercs get me to my feet, holding Millennia with their guns. Push me toward the ropes, clip me on, magpulley zips me up and out. Merc up top gets me secure. Heli uncloaks above, shudders down, get on, snap into a rumble seat. Each of the mercs zips up behind. Lead merc comes in last. Start wondering who they could be. Too professional to be corp militia. Didn't think anybody like this was still in the Commonwealth. Heli lifts off, recloaks, takes a wide path away from Cap HQ up through the Over.

Lead merc takes off his mask: Jozy Jinx. Shit.

"You did good, Run," she says. "You're very convincing with everything. I'm sure you put it all together, but damn if you didn't make it look like you hadn't. Well done."

I nod. Don't know if I'm fine or if I'm fucked. Do know that if I try anything now, I'm fucked up and down. Smile. "Yeah, but you're the real actor."

"I told you I was always watching," Jozy says. "Only way to not foul an experiment is to observe from a measured distance."

"Nice to know I'm lab material."

"You're more than that, Run," she says.

Heli skates through Avalon, Elysium, past the Loop and down to an empty parking lot in the Under. Familiar one, with a Kento sitting, looking pretty. The secret Bouq base. Jozy and the mercs unload me, guns at my back, escort me to the lift between the trash processors, pile me in. We descend.

"So, you're going to turn me into a suicide bomb," I say.

"Don't believe everything you see on a holorecord," Jozy says. "Alpha will fill you in."

"I can't wait."

nine

"Cute," I say. "Never expected to be honeypotted."

Jozy Jinx rolls her eyes, shimmer-hair glows gold. "We had to use you as a... surveillance device. Don't be a bitch about it. We fucked because I wanted to and we will again."

Maglift settles way down in the Bouq basement secret base, shudders as it stops. Doors open. Jozy and three mercs lead me down the long corridor, past the inspirational holos, young volunteers, shouting calls and hovering newsfeeds blasting stories about Noncons turning their waste into food and a lucky

Overcitier who'll step into NeonCube against the champ, Crush Mikke.

Push down the hall, all the while wondering who I'm dealing with, whether Jozy's on the up and if the Bouqs are just going to pop me the moment we get into Alpha's office. Real mindfucky, being turned into a spy camera. Got Jozy watching, Macy Lane in my head. Don't know when she'll be back, or if. Didn't go synth to become a puppet, but then maybe everything I did to survive in the Commonwealth, scraping and fighting for the cash to slink by's been puppeteering all along. Fuckier to take a beating from Hank Millennia knowing that as bad as the Cap is, the Bouqs aren't aiming higher, just softer. Should've known. Too many free lunch offers. Been better off running chips and organs, betting the Cube.

Jozy and the mercs push me into Harriett Alpha's office. Alpha rises, waves for me to take a seat. Jozy sits beside me, mercs stand against the wall, rifles up, eyes forward, stony.

"Mr. Ono-Marks, welcome back," Alpha says. "I imagine you must be pretty confused and perhaps even angry, but I assure you that everything is going to plan, and we have held your safety in the highest regard throughout this process."

Look at Jozy, she nods, smiles. "We're not dumb, Run. Promise."

"Yes, well," Alpha says, looking at Jozy. "We'd also like to extend a gesture of good faith. Miss Jinx, please."

Jozy pulls my pistol from her ballistic vest, holds it by the barrel, passes it to me. "I believe this is yours. Should've looked after it better."

Take the weapon, examine it, it's real. Pop my thigh compartment, holster it. "Thanks. Millennia beating the shit out of me was a little distracting. Won't lose sight of it again."

"We've also tracked down your Kento. It's yours when you leave here."

Alpha places both hands on the desktop, leans forward. "We probably owe you an apology. Our deception wasn't specifically to mislead you, but to create a believable series of events that would allow us to easily infiltrate Millennia's office while appearing... accidental. Miss Jinx was engaged to install subroutine recording and surveillance programs in your synth body. And our leaker, Miss Lane, was well known to us prior to your mission to ferret her out. And you did a beautiful job showing us just how far away from us she truly is. We will do what we can to remove her hacked code from your system. Honestly, we've never seen anything like the device she used to shutdown your motility, speech, and defense operations. It's remarkable, though I'm sure not to you, being the lab rat in the endeavor. Regardless, your contribution to our cause has been monumental. You got us a clear record of Millennia and the Cap's plans to turn the entire Undercity into an indoctrination prison camp. It will be impossible for them to deny, and we'll have a real shot at taking control in the elections this Fall. You have mine, and the entire Bouquet's thanks."

"Glad to help," I say. "Unfortunate that you all'll just keep things the way they are. Lane showed me a lot of information. Hard to forget."

Alpha sighs, sits down, taps at the screen on her desk and pulls up a holo. "Yes. I'm certain that Miss Lane and President Millennia didn't speak well of us. But you must understand they have their own motives." Holo lights up, displays a map of the Commonwealth and the surrounding Wastes. Colored markers, green, blue, and red litter the map. Blue in Overcity Avalon, green in the Seventh district of the Under, red in Tian, Eden. The Wastes, with points for Noncon settlements, is all blue. Looks like the map in the main room where all the kids are buzzing. "This map represents how citizens of the Commonwealth perceive the Bouquet. Green areas are generally positive, while blue are undecided, and red strongly support the Cap."

"I'm familiar with election mapping," I say. "Lane told me that you've been messing with the Noncons, setting them against the Caps and vice versa. Also showed me that the Noncons are doing just fine out there."

Harriet Alpha's face twists a bit, forces it into a smile. "A strategy of confusion has been employed when it comes to the Noncons and Cap activity in the Wastes. That's true. We are designing a narrative, Mr. Ono-Marks. All politics is narrative. The Cap wants folks to believe that without them, the people of the Over will lose everything. The Noncons want folks to believe that they don't need any governance at all, which is just... childish. And we in the Bouquet wish to show the citizens of the Commonwealth that there's a path to a brighter day, long and slow, and plodding as it may have to be, due to our opposition. Generating a false crisis in the Wastes allows us to show how we can help the Noncons—and we do, mind you, supply them with a wealth of rations and cash—as well as display the kindness we hope to imbue in folks on the newsfeed every night. That it holds the Cap back is just a pleasant side effect."

"This is a long game situation, Run," Jozy says. "We have to change folks' hearts and minds over time, and then the Commonwealth can be anything we want it to be."

"What about the folks who're caught in between now and then?" I ask.

"Rome, Mr. Ono-Marks," Alpha says, peering across her desk. "It took the Cap decades to cement their power and mold the Commonwealth in their image. It will take time, and cunning, to mold it back. We may have been naive before, but we now understand the lengths to which we must go if we expect to take leadership of this city again."

"And then?" I ask.

"And then, anything is possible. There will be a time of transition. We will listen to our corporate partners and the citizens of the city to determine the best cou—"

"Corps aren't going to be interested in upending their power," I say.

Harriet Alpha's eyes get narrower. "They will take convincing, but we are prepared to convince them."

153

"How?"

Jozy glares at me. Shimmer-hair flickers red and orange.

"The Bouquet leadership at that time will choose an appropriate course of action to bring the Corps into the fold," Harriet Alpha says. "I assure you that our hearts are in the right place, Mr. Ono-Marks. I comprehend your misgivings, and that's our fault. We betrayed your trust and put you in a compromising position. We are... learning how to compete with the Caps so that we can stop their reign of terror, and we make mistakes."

Bite my tongue. Taste some blood.

"They're good folks, Run," Jozy says. "Harriet and the rest of the Bouquet want to make the Commonwealth better, and that takes time. The fact that she's not trying to body slam you like Hank Millennia should tell you what you need to know." She leans in and whispers. "Besides, I know where all the bodies are buried. If they screw up I'll screw them."

Somehow Jozy Jinx's endorsement isn't reassuring.

"As a thank you for risking your life and limb for our gain, we're prepared to upgrade your synth parts with the PerpetMot upgrades," Alpha says. "We'd like to provide them to you tomorrow, with your consent. How does that sound?"

Too good to be true. "As long as it's the real deal," I say.

"Miss Jinx will preside over the entire procedure to ensure it," Harriet Alpha says. "For now, please show Mr. Ono-Marks to the quarters we've prepared for him. There will be time for more questions after you're permacharged, and I promise that I will answer any you have."

^^^o

Quarters are small, but plush, considering they're in a covert ops base. Bed's pretty big. Shelves run above it, down the wall beside the door. Stacks of Bouq campaign holos on the shelves, along with a collection of old books, paper and everything, mostly self-help, visualization, and pop psych. Big chronopane shows the time; 22:10, overlaid on a holowindow. Looks like an Overcity night there, five or six stories up, rooftops, skyline, starry skies with wisps of clouds. Must be longtimers working with the Bouqs here to have rooms built specifically to feel like you're not underground. Funny, the lies we tell ourselves with tech.

Jozy enters behind me, waves the other mercs away. "I've got it from here. Dismissed." Walks over to the back corner of the room, near the holowindow, taps on a panel beside it, music starts playing. Brass, warm, bold, triumphant. Never heard it before. "This'll drown out our voices. No fun in being overheard," she adds. Jozy starts taking off my jacket, helps me sit down on the bed. "Take it easy. You took some hits, not to mention how frightening that must've been. A night's rest will do you good. Then we'll get you on the table, replace your synth kit and you'll, literally, be a whole new man."

Nanos're still working hard, repairing surface weaknesses left by Hank Millennia's fists. Can feel them as a hot ball in the pit of my gut. Charge meter's at 32% drops to 31%, be at a quarter tank by morning. Nanos can't fix my black eye, gash on my cheek, bruises on my neck. That'll take a couple days the old fashioned way. "I don't like this," I say. "Don't trust Alpha. Not sure I trust you."

Jozy leans in, runs her thumb gently around the orbit of my eye, down my cheek, across my lips. "I told you not to trust anyone," she says. "You don't have to trust to work together. The Bouqs want to do good things, but they need power to do them, and that power is all tied up in a fucked up system. I don't think they'll win, Run. They don't have the guts. If they did, they wouldn't be playing the Cap's game at all. Being the better side of a shitty coin is nothing to be proud of. But if one of them has to win, the Bouqs'll at least acknowledge what needs to change."

"Hiring corp troops to kill Noncons doesn't inspire confidence that they'll acknowledge anything," I say. "And I don't care that the Caps are doing the same thing. Making it look like the Noncons are suffering, bumbling wastoids and weirdos disproves some silent morality."

"Look, Run, the Noncon thing bothers me too. I grew up thinking they were wistful hermits, chasing some misguided dreams driven by technophobia. Knowing that they're pawns in this tug-of-war between parties... it's disgusting. It's wrong. Now that we're close with Alpha, we can change that. They'll listen to us. They owe you big now."

Laugh. "They don't owe me. They're buying my silence with the PermaMot upgrade," I say. "Folks like this don't listen either. No different than the Cap.

Everyone's real warm and loving when they're winning, or think they will soon."

Jozy bends down and kisses me, slips some tongue, grips me by the ears. Shimmer-hair goes wild. "Wait and see, for me. After the procedure tomorrow, I'll get you tuned up, and we can go back to my place, lay low, see what happens. If you decide you're out, I'm out with you." Kisses me again. More tongue.

"Doubt I'll be changing my mind," I say.

"I know," she says, removing her merc gear, unzipping her jumpsuit. "Actions speak louder than words, don't they?"

Shimmer-hair flashes green. Jozy Jinx straddles me.

^^^o

"It's gotta be annoying to have everyone using you for your body... to have me in your head," Macy Lane says. "I didn't sell you to the Cap just to draw out the Bouqs. I mirrored your loc data too. They know where you are right now. They're on their way. This is war. These gov hooligans can finally destroy each other. And I can't wait to see how it plays out."

Snap awake. Not a dream. Macy Lane still in my head. The Cap is coming. Can't be much time. Chronopane reads 3:26. Look at Jozy, nude, curled around me, sleeping soundly. Hold her shoulder, shake her just a bit. "Wake up. Caps are coming. We need to leave now."

She yawns, stretches, purrs. "What? What're you —"

"Lane's still in my fucking head. Used me to tip the Caps off to this place. Said they're headed this way."

"I scanned you on the heli," Jozy says, sitting up. "You're not bugged or hacked. There's no way. Look at me." I do. Jozy gets real close, her eye is on my right eye. "Look up, as far as you can. Look down. Okay, left. Shit. Shit. Fuck. Fuck. Fuck!"

"What?" I ask, still looking left.

"Little prick," Jozy says.

"What'd the little prick do?" I ask.

"There's a little prick mark on the outside of your right eye. Lane must've put a biochip in there. Wouldn't show up on a scan, wouldn't trigger an immune response," Jozy reaches for her merc uni, roots through the vest pockets, comes back holding a

thin, cylindrical wand. "Hold still. Keep looking left."
Presses the wand to the white of my eye, triggers it.

Feels like a shot of air, a jab, then suction. Vision
goes blurry. Eye starts throbbing. "Tell me this is
almost over."

"Don't be a baby," she says. "I've almost got it.
Lane gave it cilia. The biochip keeps swimming
around in there."

Vision goes white. "What the fuck, Jozy. I can't
see."

"It'll come back. Besides, I almost have the
biochip."

Tiny fleck surrounded with little legs slides into
the middle of the white. Wriggles around like it's
doing a dance. Lane probably made it that way. Why
just inject a foreign computer into a person when you
can make it a wiseass too? "I see it. Dead center."

"I've got it. I've got it," Jozy says. Wand moves in,
biochip flutters frantic, gets sucked inside the wand.
"There." She holds the wand up, looks at it. Biochip is
magnified inside the tube. Jozy presses a tab on the
device, wave of hot white light shoots from tip to tip,
biochip pops and sizzles. "I've never seen anything
that advanced."

"Sure I'm not full of those things?" I ask.

"I've had a good look at the rest of your body," Jozy replies. "I think you're clean, so to speak."

Nod. Put on my jacket, grab a smoke, light it. "Let's get out of here."

"We should warn the others," Jozy says, climbing into her jumpsuit, zipping it up. "They're not ready for a war here. Especially one they aren't expecting."

"Long as we get to the Kento and get gone," I say.

We exit the quarters into the long circuitous corridor. Jozy starts banging on doors. I do the same. Rouse a few Bouqs who hustle to get dressed, pull whatever weapons they have out of lockers. Jozy gets her mercs moving too. Even if five against an army won't do it. Get to Alpha's quarters last. The Bouq boss takes a rifle from her bookcase, smiles, follows us into the main corridor. Alarm starts blaring. `Perimeter compromised! Perimeter compromised!` Run toward the maglift and it chimes. The lift has arrived. Doors open. Mr. Delta, dead-eyed, head tilted back, bloody mouthed. Behind him, eight PalCorp militiamen. They push Delta forward, body drops to the floor. PalCorp start firing wildly. Grab my iron, aim and fire. Hit two of them. Not fatal. One shoulder, one gut. Grab Jozy and pull her back. Alpha starts rattling off shots. Other Bouqs and mercs start firing too. Lift disappears. Cap'll send reinforcements. Pieces of ceiling start falling, chunks, big ones. Look up and see a boring bit pushing through, about two meters wide. Cap wasn't going to let the Bouqs chokepoint them. Boring bit powers down. I roll to the side, Jozy on the other as the bit stops, gate door slides open. Another eight PalCorp guys roll out. More ceiling starts falling. Enough that chunks down some of the Bouqs. Alpha keeps wasting militiamen though, crack shot. Group from the maglift is done. New bits come down. Three more. Caps'll make Swiss of the base, flood it with troops. Dive over to Jozy, fire four more shots, kneecap a couple PalCorp, hit one in the face. Blood everywhere. Not good.

"There another way out of his base?" I ask.

Jozy looks pale. "Alpha's office. There's an access hatch for an escape tunnel."

"C'mon."

Heft Jozy over my shoulder and sprint toward Alpha's office. Alpha grits her teeth and grins as we pass, keeps firing at the Caps like she enjoys it. Other Bouqs flood from the quarters, must be secrets on secrets for all the folks they have down here. Won't be a fair fight, but it'll be a fight. Maybe the Bouqs will win. Maybe not. Either way no one in the Over will talk about it. Won't make the newsfeed. Get into Alpha's office, set Jozy down. She winces. Blood seeps from her chest. "Pull the shelf, code is 9329," she says.

Do it. Access hatch reveals and opens. "How'd you?"

"I'm always watching," she says, coughs.

Pick her up again and climb into the shaft. Big enough to stand up, built for expeditious exits. Sprint at full speed for what feels like an hour. Battle behind us gets quieter, finally falls silent. Not even a pinging echo of a gunshot. Just my feet striking the metal floor. Jozy's blood runs down my jacket, drips from my lapels.

"Where's this tunnel go?" I ask.

"Outside," is all she says.

Set her down, open my forearm compartment, pull first aid chems, some thread. Shoot her up, find the wound, stitch it quickly. Still bleeding, but less. Scan her vitals. Weak, but there. Have to get her somewhere soon. Tunnel doesn't seem to end. No light equals no end. Carry her forward, disoriented. No idea where we are. Can't get a sense with my internal compass. Tunnel might be magshielded. Another thirty minutes. Forty. Scan her vitals. Weak, but there. Wonder how the Bouqs are holding up. No footsteps

163

tailing us must be a good thing. It's the war Macy Lane wanted, at least. Not a slaughter. Charge meter chimes. 10%. Can't let Jozy down. Not dying in here. Push on, dust starts kicking up, a breeze, trickle of water in the bottom of the tunnel. Still no light. Look around, panicked, has to be a door here somewhe—A hatch, meter wide, corroded, water seeping in, mud slipping through.

Lower Jozy to the floor. She sighs. Doesn't say anything. Press against the hatch. Jammed. Shit. Pop open my right index, activate the cutting laser, start tearing through the door. More mud and water. Jozy breathing faintly, blood seeping. Laser slices the hatch, I punch it open. Charge meter chimes. 5% remaining. Feed Jozy through the opening, climb through after her. She was right. We're outside. Of the Commonwealth. The Wastes stretch out before us. City wall is a klick back. In the distance, see a plume of steam rising, a collection of conical roofs. Noncon settlement. Has to be. Sling Jozy across my shoulders, start walking. Air is cleaner than I expected. No burn. Acid must be light today. Sun beats down. Dust rolls in waves that crash against us, clawing us as they bend back to start again. Legs start weakening, seizing up. Diagnostic has nanos all over the place, clearing dust jams, bailing muck and water. Sucking my charge dry. 3%. Noncon settlement seems like it keeps moving away. Can't be. Wastes cause illusions, heat and flat land. Fact that I'm gassed doesn't hurt. Walk on until I can't anymore. Charge meter flickers. 1%. Standby mode coming. Set Jozy down carefully. Kiss her on the forehead. Eyes don't open. Blood around the stitches is crusty. Sit beside her. Take her hand.

"I'm sorry," I say. "Sure you are too." Lay down. "Least we didn't die in there."

ten

Sky is pink, ground is purple. Green fog rolls across the Wastes, wraps around me like fingers gripping. New acid jazz wafts on the waves of dust that crash into me, turn to water droplets, roll down my body casting colorful light prismatically. Breathe and the air is thick, sweet. Move and the air is dense, muddy, slowing me down. Jozy, naked, stands about twenty meters away. Shimmer-hair on strobe, can't see her face clearly, silhouette keeps shifting. Now she's Harriet Alpha, machine gun at her hip, cigar clenched between her teeth, stench of blood. Barrel flash obscures her, can't be sure. Looks like her, but where am I? Then Macy Lane, cackling, waving holos around herself in a mad swirl, conducting it to the beat with her fingers, mouth full of razors. "I'm inside. I'm INSIDE!" Heart racing. Try to run at her, can't. Now it's Hank Millennia, hands balled, veins pulsing, arms surging, teeth gritted. Can hear them grind, stone set on stone. Millennia sees me. Think so. Can't see his eyes. Just a glint of light where the face should be. Massive form charges at me, head down, fists raised. Put up my hands. Can't move fast enough. It slams me to the ground.

Fists don't hurt. Keep coming at me, but nothing. Each strike turns to water, splashes away. Try to focus, Millennia isn't even there. Just orange sky turning pink turning purple. A weight on my abdomen. Something moving there. Tiny proddings. Hard to sit up, takes all my strength. Crane my neck, see a gray pile of fuzz, whiskers, big ears. Kneads its paws into my gut, body starts going shimmer, flashing every color, some colors I can't even make out. Little feet keep stomping into me, over and over, fast beat, doesn't hurt, just feels... Don't know how. Just keeps tapping, so much we start to sink. Ground rises. Feels warm, soupy. Push down through it, out the other side, whatever that is. Now I'm suspended in the sky.

Kaleidoscope envelopes. Ground below is green, orange, blue, silver. Then red, wet. Muddy. Bloody. Little feet push me toward the muck, a stir of filth and blood. Try to push back, paddle against the air. Nothing. Little gray fuzz sends me through it. Feel comfort, then surprise, fear, terror... Push through a... fleshy barrier. The other side, everything is clear, sunny. Birds chirping. Grass and trees. Shadow falls across my face.

"Sometimes the best way to get clean is to get dirty," the Chinchilla says.

"What?" I say.

"I can't tell you what to think. I can only remind you how."

"Get off me." Swing my arm at the Chinchilla. It disappears. Reappears on my head.

"Breathe. You have to. You'll never solve the mystery if you don't," it says.

"What mystery? The Caps and Bouqs?"

"No, silly. Yourself."

^^^o

Electricity courses through me. Eyes open, blurry, thick with sleep, dry. Cough. Jolt up. Arms, legs, everything's still here. Reddish hue of the Wastes, blue-gray sky, gentle breeze tossing grains of sand. Run diagnostics. Nanos still working. Systems at full op. Charge meter reads 28%, then 29, 30. Faster than I've seen. Report shows no major damage, just temp limits to joint functionality, athletic capacity. No memory corruption. Wire plugged into my abdomen, runs over my shoulder to a... battery. Classic tech, Caesium Ion. Size of a carton of smokes. Must be thirty years old. Hot to the touch. Its screen shows 70% charge. Someone hooked me up to an old car batt.

Jozy. Where is she? Look all around. Just a stain of blood soaked sand and shale. No body. No tracks. Animal didn't drag her. Something moved her, lifted her. Long shadow falls across me. Spin around. Tall hooded figure, gray beard hanging below the collar. Long metal staff in his hand. Steps closer, pulls back the hood. Face is weathered, but youthful, eyes hidden behind dark goggles.

"You looked like you needed the juice more than I," he says. "This should keep you going for a couple of weeks if you're careful. We'll get it mounted to your synth parts now that you're up and around."

"Who are you?" Pop my thigh compartment, grab the gun. "Where's Jozy?"

169

"I am Darius Spinks, elder of the Unbound Community, which is to say that I've been with Us the longest," he says. "You can put *that* away. Your friend is in our medical facility receiving care as we speak. She lost a lot of blood, but we have talented surgeons in whom I hold great confidence."

"You're Noncons," I say.

Darius Spinks chuckles. "That's what we're called, anyway. Dangerous stuff when you're identified solely by what you're not. We don't fear conformity. The UC is a place of laws and justice and love and camaraderie. We simply reject the statutes of living that the Commonwealth holds most dear. Now, if you're strong enough, rise to your feet, and I will show you to your friend."

Standing takes some doing. Legs weak from nanos still working hard on internal repairs. Get to my feet, cable to my gut stretches taut. Bend down, pick up the battery, heavy. Elbows and wrists getting repaired too. Peer at Spinks. He smiles.

"Good. Let's get going. Storms will be coming soon," he says, then strides forward, planting his staff with each step, in the direction of the rising steam I'd seen before I shutdown.

Follow Spinks for twenty meters onto a well-manicured trail, almost a road. How'd I miss it before? Spinks flicks the side of his staff, slides his thumb, beacon of light glows at the tip. `Travel shield activated. User Authorized: Darius Spinks.` Whole road glows, magshield canopy slides over it, forming a tunnel. Shield closes behind us as we move, extends in front of us. "Storms?" I say. "Acid rains, you mean?"

Spinks eyes me and laughs. "No. There's no acid rains out here. Just toxic dust storms when the northerly wind catches the edge of the Commonwealth, lifts the irradiated dirt below the pollution condensers and carries it this way."

"Couldn't you just move?"

"The UC is built on the only source of fresh water for miles," Spinks says. "Tapped a well into the aquifer. Dense stone below filters out the toxins better than a HomeCom six-phase. We tested it. Easier to stay here, deal with the storms. Temp shields like this one protect each structure, otherwise we live with the environment we're given." A roar shakes the ground. Spinks points toward the Commonwealth with his staff. "Here it comes. Be calm. Just keep walking with me."

Huge rolling plume of yellow-green gas and dust stands up like a cobra just outside the Commonwealth wall. Swirls in the air, towering ten stories or more, tumbles under its own size, falls like a poorly demoed tower, toppling, spraying, crashing toward us. Hits the ground, everything shakes, then it's just a dense wall of yellow-green too thick to see through barrelling toward us. Hits the magshield hard enough it shakes. Stumble, catch myself. Hail of sand and poison echoes around us. Spinks turns to check on me. Can't hear him over the noise, wave him off, keep walking. Storm surrounds us for the rest of the walk. Can't see where we're going. Trusting Spinks not to lead us astray. Old man seems to know the way.

Before long he stops, waves for me to stand beside him. I step up. "We've arrived. Stay close at my side while we step from shield to shield. I'd hate for your joints to get gummed up again." Spinks touches the side of his staff again, slides his thumb. Light on the tip changes from green to yellow. "Now, step forward. Quickly." We do. Gust of storm hits me, knocks me sideways. Spinks grabs my jacket collar, hefts me in and forward. Quickly slides his thumb again. Staff light goes red, small light above the door of the building goes green. "Passing shield to shield requires the partial lowering of each. I apologize for not warning you adequately. I forget these things sometimes."

"That's fine," I say. Behind us the storm rages, but a sliver of blue sky and clear air starts to open, closer to the Commonwealth gates. In front, dual metal doors slide open. Encased glass cylinder sits at the center of the room, four or five folks in white smocks, holomasks huddled around a medtable. Tables and chairs surround the cylinder. Small group of teenage kids sitting there, watching the cylinder. Couple mechs buzz about, one sanitation, one recording a holo. Three of the smocked folks step away from the table. One touches a screen inside the cylinder. Comm activates. "It's a success. Students, please log the serial from the record mech and review the holo for an exam tomorrow."

Spinks raises his staff, points at the doc on the comm. "Wonderful!" Turns to me. "As I said, your friend Jozy will be just fine."

"Can I see her?"

"Not just yet. The medteam needs to keep the area sterile while the nanos complete their work," Spinks says. "Dr. Olypha can answer any questions you have. Kala, this is the other wounded traveler. As you

173

suspected, the power cell did the trick. Would you mind giving us a quick summary of the surgery you performed?"

Doc sidles up beside us, deactivates the holomask, extends a hand. "Not often we have Commonwealthers in our shop, and this was a unique opportunity to save a life and teach the class about organic reconstruction," she says. "I'm Kala Olypha, medteam for the UC."

Take her hand. "Run Ono-Marks. Thanks for taking care of her."

"It is what we do," she says smiling. "And as I said, how exciting to use the organic reconstructor on several major organs at once. We successfully regened the heart, spleen, liver, and a portion of damaged lung. I'd ask how your friend arrived at such a state, but we try to stay out of others' affairs."

"Crossfire between the Cap and the Bouqs," I say.

Kala Olypha lowers her eyes. "Yes. Tragic what happens in the Commonwealth."

"They've both been messing with you Nonco—the UC too."

Dr. Olypha frowns, looks at Spinks. He places a hand on my shoulder. "We have suffered trials, but we prefer to learn and look forward," he says. "Failing to tend to past wounds, and the belief that power alone will heal them, is why the Commonwealth is destroying itself."

"Not fast enough," I say.

"Tut tut," Spinks says. "We do not wish their destruction, but their enlightenment. It is a pity that they must find the latter only through the former. We had hoped to lead by example, and yet one side sees cruelty and exclusion as power, and the other envisions themselves capable of repurposing cruelty as kindness by distributing insignificant gifts. If the Cap and the Bouquet were capable of transcending what they perceive as strength, the Commonwealth would be a very different place indeed."

"They want control more than they want to lead," Dr. Olypha says.

"Yes. But they no longer understand what it is they wish to control," Spinks says. "They believe the Commonwealth is something that exists without its peoples, yet they will transcend it if it fails to serve them."

"The corps aren't helping either," I say.

"Indeed. They seem to believe they're self-sustaining, when in reality, they are illusions existing solely because the people continue to believe." Spinks stares into space for a moment, clears his throat. "Enough of this morbid talk. Kala, would you mind terribly showing our guest around the grounds? This should afford your friend a bit more time to recover, and you can learn more about the UC."

Nod, look at Dr. Olypha. "Lead on, doc."

"My pleasure."

Outside, storm has cleared. No more magshields, just paved paths with cart tracks down their centers. Built to move heavy equipment easily in blustery conditions. Med building sits at the center of the Unbound Community. Paths extend off of it in eight directions, each with its own access door. Looks like three of them don't see much use, given the drifts of sand. At three o'clock, a quintet of towers grow out of the Wastes, all the same. Housing for the Noncons. At noon, a promenade with a large crystal atrium at its center. "This is our commerce center and meal hall. We all gather there to eat, and to make trades of wares or of skills, as well as welcoming the handful of outsiders who pass through on their way to the Commonwealth and other megacities," Dr. Olypha says. "Over there, is our education facility." Points to ten o'clock. A cubic cement building with tall, narrow windows, and the phrase *sapientia et veritas* carved into its facia. "And our sustainable farming, and energy buildings..." Points to seven and eight. First, a group of domes filled with greenery, and second a small shack surrounded by solar panels and geopumps. "The rest is storage. We've had to be prepared for droughts, and saboteurs."

"This is nothing like what they show on the newsfeeds."

Dr. Olypha smiles and nods. "Indeed. We see the content from the Commonwealth and have long given up on advocating for accurate representation. A story in which we're failing and the Commonwealth fights over who will be our saviors is far more valuable than the truth." She laughs. "And honestly, I don't know if we'd be able to welcome all the folks who'd come if they knew how we live."

"Starting to think I should," I say.

"Yes, well, that's a discussion to have with Mr. Spinks and the other elders. Let's get you to Energy now, and get that battery properly mounted so you don't have to keep carrying it around, hmm? They might even give it another little boost."

Forgot somehow, but still holding the Caesium power pack in my hand. Check my charge. 88%. Nanos done working. Diagnostic is clean. All systems go. Nod at Dr. Olypha and follow.

Walk takes twenty minutes. Have to flip my hood, activate suntech as we approach. Glare off the solar panels is intense. Gentle hum of the geopumps is comforting. Dr. Olypha touches her fingertip to a screen beside the small shack's door. Door slides open. Room is roughly thirty square meters, lined with control panels, small corner bathroom, pong table, four chairs. Holos on the panels show solar intake status, geopump flow range. One has NeonCube records. Another blares cortexhop so loud that Dr. Olypha immediately storms toward it and turns the volume down. "Martin? You here? We need your expertise," she says.

Under the pong table, a heavy, coveralled man rolls out, rubs his eyes, stands. "Kala, what's that? I was napping."

"We have a visitor from the Commonwealth who needs your help mounting his new battery pack to his synth body." She points at me.

Hold up the pack, shake the wires. "If we can secure these connectors too..."

Martin bites his lower lip, blinks. "Yep. Not a problem. Hop on the table, champ." He pats the pong

178

table and grins. "Jared, tools." Hear a distant pixelated bark. Mechdog bounds in, toolkit gripped in its jaws. Sits in front of Martin, metal tail wagging, waits for Martin to take the kit, then starts sniffing around me on the table, paws up, muzzle in my face, actuators whirring. Buries its nose into my side, sniffing my jacket. "Delicious?" it says. "Delicious?" Martin pats the robot on the head. "Good, Jared. No delicious. Delicious later." The mechdog looks genuinely disappointed, lowers itself off the pong table, does two spins and curls up on the floor.

"Spoiled him with treats," Martin says. "How could I not with that face."

The mechdog's smooth metallic head perks, looks at me. Lifelike enough, with time, you'd almost see what Martin means. Hulking man sidles over, studies me, the battery pack, reaches down to Jared, takes up a tool. Pokes at me with a spanner. "All synth, huh? How's that treating you?"

"I've got a car battery tethered to my gut just so I can stay alive," I say.

"Quit complaining," he says. "You could be carrying extra el-bees like me. It's no picnic. Front or back?"

Shoot him a look.

179

"You want the battery mounted to the front or the back?"

"Back."

Martin nods, hums in agreement. "Jared, gimme the ten milli, the twelve milli, and that dual node energy transmit kit." Mechdog pulls the proper-sized bits, passes them up in its mouth, scampers across the room to fetch where Martin points. "Turn over," Martin says. Comply, feel prods in my back as tools dig, bore and jab. Smell melting synth skin. Hear Martin muttering curses, the clatter of tools on the table, the rhythmic rumble of Jared the mechdog watching its master work. "Alright. You're done," Martin says. "Got it as slim as I could. Energy 'mit kit will send it to you when you need it. No more wires. Charged the pack, too. Should give you a week without needing a standard charge. Just don't overload it."

"Overload it?"

"The pack isn't built to overclock its output rate, if you try to take too much juice at once, it'll overload. Then... boom."

"Understood. Not looking to press my luck," I say. Sit up and climb off the pong table. "What do I owe you?"

Martin smirks. "Nothing. Parts I had lying around. Do something nice for somebody."

Jared the mechdog sits before me, wags its metal tail. Pat it on the head. Robot coos. Check my charge meter, reading 100% now. Diagnostics are clean, all checks. Nanos are almost recharged. Hope I don't need them again soon. Put my jacket back on, pull a smoke, light it, look at Martin, already digging through some other pile of junk. Give him a nod, exit.

Return to the med building, Jozy's convalescing on a bed in the outer ring around the center op room. No sign of Dr. Olypha. Other medteam buzzing around, tending to broken bones, a cough, some vomit. Nothing serious.

"Run," Jozy calls. "What the shit. Holy shit, what the shit." Looks all around the room.

I smile. "Yeah. Noncons have it better than inside the Commonwealth."

"You saved my life."

Shake my head. "Not really. I tried. Lucky that Spinks found us. These are the folks to thank."

"Either way. Thank you. You could've left me... after I set you up, got you all caught up in this mess," she says.

"You did what you thought was right," I say.

181

Jozy looks down, watches the outer layer of her skin mend itself in real time. "I did what I thought made sense, but the war that's brewing doesn't serve anyone but the Caps and Bouqs. I don't want anything else to do with them. I just want out. I need a reset."

"Soon as we get back to the Commonwealth, you can hunker down at your flat," I say. "I have an idea to deal with the Cap and Bouquet, once and for all. Then I'll join you. We can start over."

"I can't go back. They'll find me and they'll kill me," she says. "I'm going to stay here. I cleared it with Spinks. They'll let me stay, until the chaos dies down."

"Good," I say. Heart cracks. "Keep an eye on me from here. Cover my tracks, cover your own. Make sure Macy Lane isn't still pulling the strings somewhere," I say.

She watches the wound in her chest continue to mend, bridging her sternum, filling and smoothing her skin. Shimmer-hair observes in somber blue-gray. Looks up at me, tears in her eyes. "I'll be watching. I want you back with me, Run. I'm fond of you."

"I'm fond of you too."

Spinks leads me out of the Untethered Community. At the edge of the UC, Spinks hands me a bag heavy with water, food supplies, points off toward the Commonwealth, a shiny silver mound in the distance. "No storms predicted for at least 36 hours. Plenty of time for you to return to the city. You have our love and best wishes for your safety, from the entire UC. And I hope that our paths will cross again."

Nod. "They will. I'm coming back for her."

"And we will do right by her until you do. Miss Jinx is a wonderfully capable addition to our community," he says. "Go in peace."

eleven

March toward the Commonwealth, jacked on Caesium car batt juice, watching the metallic glimmer of civilization grow larger, brighter by the klick. Air is clear. Multiple scans return normal atmospheric comp, save for the extra ozone that keeps the Wastes toasty, and dry. Clouds swirl overhead. It's desolate, but not nearly as bad as the Commonwealth would tell you. If I didn't have something to do, living out here with Jozy'd be just fine, especially considering the UC's setup. Walk's boring, though. Nothing to see but expanse and the mess of the city. Nothing to think about but getting back in, dealing with the Cap and

Bouqs, finding a way back. Only complication is dust clogging my synth joints. Nanos're taking care of it, but the grinding is annoying to hear. Pop my forearm panel and check the newsfeeds.

Every story's about a mysterious explosion and fire in the Fourth. "Tragedy in the Undercity, as four storage buildings and a sanitation mech house exploded and burned. Authorities in the Cap, Bouquet and their corporate partners are currently investigating the event, which all of them called, 'Troubling.'" Footage of burning buildings, rubble everywhere, a Kento M6 rained with ash in an adjacent parking lot. My Kento. Gotta be. Looks in decent condition from the vid. Worth a look when the attention dies down. "Fortunately, no one was hurt in the blast and conflagration, as the Fourth District is unpopulated. Still, Commonwealth officials, and citizens in both the Overcity and Undercity have expressed concern that the disaster might have been the result of stresses on the environmental systems or on the notably decaying infrastructure of the Undercity. Our team will investigate all possibilities and bring all discoveries to light. And now a message from our sponsors at PalCorp..." Feed changes to a PalCorp militia helping an elderly Overcitier across the street somewhere in Avalon. Big cover up in place. City can make hundreds of bodies disappear. Explosions and fire makes it go away. Having a dumping ground like the Undercity makes it simple. Wonder if Alpha survived, other Bouq kids. Improbable, but no covert op is without multiple escape plans. Me and Jozy might've used Alpha's office hatch, but there'd have to be others. Easier to put an end to all of it if they didn't make it. More blood to answer for. PalCorp ad ends, slides into a spot for the next ep of NeonCube. Hank Millennia appears, dressed in his old costume—a singlet covered in prox spikes—grins into the feed. "As we all question the horrific explosion that took place in the Undercity, I have decided to return to the Cube as special referee to demonstrate that the Cap, its partners, and the Commonwealth remain strong!" Flexes and the prox spikes extend around him in a prickly aura. "We must continue to live our lives, to fight to win! Join me, if you've got the guts, in the

Cube!" Turn the feed off. Nothing but bluster. At least Millennia's worried he might lose folk's faith. Wouldn't do the image work if he wasn't.

Walk another hour, two. Nanos keep the joints moving, if rough. City wall rises up over me, casts a shadow across the sand. Only spot that isn't dark is the fresh dump of radiation mingling with the grains just below the exhaust pipes. Should work to get me back in, direct to the Under, somewhere in the First between the fabricators and liquid and solid waste dumps. Nothing but the best for Run Ono-Marks. Approach the irradiated sands, notable for their orange-pink glow. Flip up the hood, drop the mask. HUD monitors the rad level: 210, 211. Keeps climbing as I get closer. Mask should protect the only parts of me still vulnerable, at least for as long as I'll be wading in it. Heavier waste piled among the sand's the bigger concern, hard to keep footing. Exhaust pipes loom, five huge maws, two actively spewing trash, radioactive particle waste. Other three liquid and solid. Slurry burbles and churns, but the rad-heavy powder floats up top, kicks around with every gust careening off the Commonwealth exterior.

Wade in, floor's uneven, old appliances, comms, mechs, compacted cubes of household refuse, all slippery with piss, shit, oil, grease, and decomposing organics. Tap the wrist screen, activate balance control. Nanos focus on keeping joints steady, maximizing pliability. Happy not to have human legs right now, each step a cause for tetanus or worse. Knee high now, about one-third of the way to the pipes. Set my sights on the trash tube, least messy and toxic option. Push forth. Charge meter reads full, still pulling from the pack on my back. Toxic swamp is up to my waist. Ground feels more compacted, sturdy. Just a few more meters and I'm there.

Bodies start pouring out of the trash tube, dozens. Nude, no ID, bloody. Must be from the siege on the Bouq secret base. Charge ahead, try to catch them as they slide out, sink into the rad pit. Get my hands on one. Grab the body by the wrist, heft it up out of the muck, wipe the face clean. Harriet Alpha. Riddles with burns and bullet wounds, notable marks on her cheeks on either side of her mouth. Torture's my guess. The Cap won the battle, took a prize. Whether Alpha gave up the Bouqs or not wouldn't matter. Macy Lane did that for them. Torture had to be for the fun of it. Millennia sending a message to the Bouq leadership that mercy was off the table. Drag Alpha's body out of the pit and lay it on the sands of the

Wastes. Go back for others, can't be sure who's who without ID. PalCorp and Bouq volunteers in there. Pull ten more out, lay them alongside Alpha. Take a moment to consider that I might be the only person in the Commonwealth to mourn them in person. Any fam couldn't come forward without the Cap making life hell. This fucking city. This fucking life.

Trudge back to the waste pipe, watching for bodies, heavy trash, and climb in. Echo in the tube's a good sign, nothing coming. Follow it twenty-five meters, well clear of the width of the exterior and interior walls, flip open the ring finger on my right hand, turn on the torch, start cutting away. Circle of metal slips loose, grab it, pull it inside the tube. Nice and quiet. Poke my head out into the First.

Industrial sector's bustling with mechs, folks acting as mech supervisors, screens in hand checking levels, adjusting inputs and outputs. Commonwealth's production and waste systems're mostly automated. Prerogative: make more stuff, get rid of old stuff. Timeline: immediate and constant. Folks aren't paying attention to me as I slink out of the waste pipe and shake what trash and irradiated slurry I can from myself. HomeCom and LyfTek plants hum, faint pleasant music wafts from inside them, something to keep the folks working from wondering about not. All the unused screens, hologear, furnishings being created just to be created, that'll wait for enough folks in the Over to abandon the old and update or upgrade, and the former will find its way to the tube, slip into the slurry to rot and decay. Always room for more. Never room for just enough. PerpetMot facility's the busiest. Mechs flying in and out, staffers working banks of screens inside. Can't tell exactly what they're doing, but the company moniker is all you need to know. Still going to take the synth upgrade if I can get my hands on it. I'm no idiot.

Trip through the First is quicker than I'd expected, darkness of the Under is my friend. First butts up to the Ninth, just have to hop a couple light sec fences to get in. No one living in the Ninth is important to the Over, this is where folks like me are hidden, and the systems built to protect us are faulty or designed to protect them from us.

^^^o

No security at my building. Take the maglift to my apartment, door's closed, scan to get in. Place is ransacked. Screens torn off the wall, couch flipped, bed cut open, foam everywhere. Someone's been here, and I've got a couple sharp starting guesses. Scan the room. Boot depressions on the rug by the couch. Scuffs on the polyplast floor in the kitchen. Drawers pulled out, junk spilled everywhere. Don't have much, don't need much with a synth body. Looks like the anti-grav series of NeonCube crossed with a trashmech explosion. Might've brought some of their own shit in here just to leave it. Nice to know I'm wanted at least.

Slide over to the shelves beside the cracked big screen and the holoprojector. Tap three times, draw a triangle with my index finger. Shelf slides up, reveals the surveillance screen I installed. Whole place is eyes. Easy enough to rig, and hard to expect. Never thought I'd really need it. Records for the day will show anyone who came in. Only the tedious task of scanning through it. Watch as five ops in plain clothes pop the door without issue, must be a hacker among them. Look around dumb for a few minutes, probably surprised at how small the place is, how little there is to find. They must've expected me to be the packrat type, logging all my gigs on a harddrive or discs and then using them as coasters like a fucking idiot. Punks root through everything, tear it all up. Out of frustration. No order or urgency. Looks like they're enjoying it. Just thrashing my shit because they could. Amateurs. One of them takes out a pen, writes something down, leaves the note on the kitchen counter.

Cross the room to the note. `Mr. Ono-Marks, One more job and the Cap will forget the whole thing. Refuse, and we'll do to you what we've done to your place.` No signature. Not the writer type, clearly. But the string of words did form a thought. Cap's still interested in my services. Not at all suspicious.

Back to the surveillance screen, punks finish tearing up my stuff, sit on the couch for a bit, vape themselves stupid. One of them falls asleep. Another paces around nervous, tapping his foot, waving his arms. Probably yelling at the others to get up and take shit seriously... the guy could come home any minute. The vaper waves it off. Nah. We're cool, man. Relax a minute. Scan forward, punks're just sitting for a while, half an hour. Then the nervous one gets up, goes to the bathroom. Scan forward. Never comes out. Others finally get up, pound on the door, jump around like idiots. Mocking the one in the can. That door jams sometimes. Have to really dig in and pull it open if it

192

does. Double over laughing and leave. Leave the nervous punk inside, in my bathroom. Wonders never cease.

Go to the bathroom door, press my ear against it. Snoring. That's some shit right there. Dig my hands into the doorjamb, get a fingertip grip on the edge of the door, put all my synth might into it. Door unjams, rotors catch, it slips into its pocket in the wall. Poor little bee-and-eee's fast asleep. Can't be comfortable sleeping sitting up on a toilet. Just a baby, probably eighteen or twenty, pale and blond. My bets on Undercity kid looking for some easy cash. Vape must've tuckered him out. Probably started freaking because of the chem and the door jam, got sleepy after the adrenal rush wore off. Unwelcome guest, either way. Pop the thigh compartment, grab the gun, put it on him.

"Wake up," I say. "Time for school, kiddo!"

Little tyke doesn't rile. Tap him on the face with the gunbarrel. Lets out a little mumble.

"Time to wake up," I yell, winding the iron up so it emits a shrill hum.

That does it. Kid blinks stupidly, eyes go wide, face twists up. Struggles to pull his pants on. "Don't kill me. Please don't kill me. Please," is all he can muster.

Step back out of the bathroom, keep the aim on him. Kid's paler than he was, probably'd piss his pants if he hadn't already emptied. "What're you doing in my place?" I ask.

Trips on his own pants, stumbles, starts crying. "We were supposed to send you a message. Please, don't shoot me. I don't want to die."

"Who's we? The other four technopricks who left you in here, and trashed my stuff?"

Kid nods. Sobs. "We got a gig to intimidate you. You weren't here," he says. "So they said we should mess stuff up and wait for you. Send a message. Please don't kill me."

Keep the iron on him. "Not too kind to mess my stuff up. Betting the Cap didn't ask you to do that. Was it your idea?"

Kids shakes his head so hard his hair spikes flop side to side. "No, sir. I wanted to leave the note and go."

Nod. Lower the gun. "You had the right idea. Though you shouldn't've broken in here in the first place. Here's the deal. I won't kill you, but you have to take a message to the Cap for me. Sound good?"

Kid nods. "Yes. I can do that. Please just don't kill me."

Smile. "You tell the Cap that I'm in. I'll do their one more job. They can expect to hear from me later today."

"Okay. I'll tell them," the kid says.

"Thanks. Be careful out there, coming down from a chem vape might leave you disoriented. I want my message delivered. You got me?"

Kid confirms and beats feet out of my place.

Spend a few minutes cleaning up the mess. Sit down and record a couple of holos. Grab a clean jacket from the closet. Saddle up.

^^^o

Akari's shop in the Seventh has a defense shield around it. Must be with a client or just feeling extra paranoid. Whole district's deserted as usual. Even the corps out looking to shake folks down have gone home, or been called back to protect Cap and Bouq resources. Drop my hood, deactivate the incog, when I get to her door. Cam picks me up right away, swivels, looks me up and down.

"Thank cash it's you, Run," Akari says. "C'mon in."

Cam swivels back to its standard position, defense shield flickers, opens just enough for me to slip through, Akari's door follows suit. The shop's a mess. Charging table is pushed to the corner, tools are all over the place, synth parts are piled like cordwood in the middle of the room, cabinets are open, her main screen is cracked, still flickering. Newsfeed on it's difficult to make out until the same explosion and fire footage plays. Chyron proves they're still spreading the official line.

"Are you alright?" I ask. "What the hell happened?"

"What do you mean 'what happened'?" she says, standing up from behind the stack of parts. "There was a huge explosion."

"I know," I say. "I was there for part of it. Long story. I meant what happened here?"

Akari waves a synth arm at me. "After that bomb went off some of the punks down here got ideas. They broke in, held me at knifepoint, took a bunch of shit, so I'm doing inventory." She gestures to the pile of synth. "Ripped the power supply out of the charging table, too. It'll take a few days to fix. I hope you don't need a charge."

Pat my back. "Not today. Got backup."

She frowns. "I thought you didn't want the extra weight. I'd've given you a batt pack."

"Didn't have any choice. Noncons set me up with it."

Akari cocks her head. "And? You're not going to expand on that?"

Light a smoke. "I was getting to it. Are you okay?"

She nods. "Nothing some time and a good defense shield won't fix. More pissed than anything. I've been here six years. Never bothered those wastoids. First sign of disorder and they pounce? I hate this fucking city."

Drag. "It's a theme. How would you feel about being part of making it better?"

"If you just picked up a gig selling HomeCom comfort offset, I'm not interested. Disgusts me when the corps feign charity in their adbuys."

"Nothing like that," I say. "I want to take the Caps and the Bouqs down. Hard reset." Drag.

"Seriously, Run," she says. "What happened to you?"

"Got a taste of both approaches. Saw them start a secret war against each other. Saw them cover it up, pretend it was a warehouse explosion. Had to escape to the Wastes. Noncons fixed me up, showed me their community," I say. "Bouqs and Caps wanted to use me against each other. I'm just looking for a way to make that happen."

She nods. "So... it wasn't an accident, the fire."

Shake my head.

"I fucking knew it!" Akari walks over to her cracked screen, slaps it to turn it off. "This fucking city."

"Our city," I say. "Will you help me?"

She scratches her head with a synth hand. Looks at it absently. "You're still pretty short on the details, Run."

"I'll catch you up once it's done," I say. "Don't want you caught up in it more than you have to be."

"Convenient," Akari says. "You're somehow wrapped up in a secret war of the Commonwealth's governing parties, went outside the city into the toxic Wastes, and all you can give me is some patriarchal 'I just wanna protect you' bullshit?"

"Look, Akari, it's serious. Both parties want to end the other. They were going to blow my synthass up to do it. I just want to give them both what they asked for. That's why I need you."

"Need me?"

"Your skillset," I say. "Some creative synth construction."

"What're you getting at?" she asks.

Drag. Smile. "They both wanted to make me into a bomb, so I figured I'd give them each one of me to do it."

"You want a synth copy of yourself?" Akari says. "And then you're going to blow it and yourself up."

Tap the tip of my nose.

"You know that'll kill you, right?"

Pace. Drag. "It'll take out the Bouqs, the Cap, and their corp lackeys too. A hard reset will make this city better. Maybe folks'll look to the Noncons for an example."

Akari shakes her head, looks down at the pile of synth limbs.

"Can you do it?" I ask.

She coughs. "Of course I can do it. The question is if I'll do it."

"Fair. What'll it take?"

"Get me out of here. Take me to the Noncons," she says.

"Bet," I say. "Small problem. After I blow up, there won't be a me to take you."

"Then don't blow up," Akari says.

Laugh. "It's not that easy. They're expecting me. One fake is doable. Two? Nah."

"You've been on this charging table every week for eight years," she says. "I can make two more of you. You won't even know which one is you when I'm done." She points a synth arm at me, shakes it.

"Be back tomorrow afternoon. If you got them done, I'll take them both. If not, I'll get you outside the city before."

She nods. "You won't be disappointed."

Smile, walk toward the door. "I can't be."

^^^◻

Walking to the Fourth takes me two hours. Chronopanes light my way, remind me that it's almost LyfTek LoCal Alcoholic Relaxation Hour. PalCorp barricades line the streets. Not many troops though. Seems the need for showy response has come and gone. Former Bouq secret HQ is off-limits. Patrol drones zip around the sky, flashing lights and cams at windows, the street, bombed out sanitation mechs scorched and still. On approach, activate cloak, flip the hood, go as stealthy as possible. Drones shouldn't pick me up unless I do something dramatic. Handful of troops are already cracking brews, won't worry about me, a funny shaped sanimech waddling about. Open my forearm screen and ping the Kento. If it's in less than a thousand pieces I'll find what's left of it.

Two blocks down, in a familiar empty lot, a pingback. The Kento. My Kento. Still cloaked, sitting right where the Bouqs, where Jozy more likely left it. Hiding in plain sight. Walk my invisible synth ass to my invisible car. Lift the gullwing, settle in, tap the screen. An old message from Jozy, created before the Bouq HQ blew: "Hey Run, sorry we got you caught up in a mess," she says. "As an apology, we fixed everything on this car, and I did a deep sweep and memory wipe for other bugs. Macy Lane won't be tracking you. No one will. Just try to stay out of trouble." Message ends, screen goes dark. Boot the Kento, pull it slowly out of the lot. Keep it under 10 kph and the cloak'll stay cloaked, unless you look right at it. PalCorp troops nearby are all chattering, grabbing each other's asses, taking pics in front of the bombed out wreckage. Kento rolls off the lot, onto the street. Make a beeline for the Loop, watching the screen closely for checkpoint pings on the map. Takes an extra twenty to avoid any corp gates and get out of the Fourth. Further you go, the less it looks like anything happened at all. That's the goal of any good cover up, to quickly generate forgetfulness. And nobody remembers shit in the Commonwealth.

Once on the Loop, I pop the Kento into sixth and cruise up into the Over, around Avalon, Elysium, Eden and Tian, and jump off at Ambrosia. The shining jewel of governance in the Overcity is a flickering flood of holos, tall living towers, and Republic Park, the sprawling promenade on which Cap and Bouq official party offices sit on opposite ends. In the center, the Commonwealth Admin Offices. The center of the gov. Came through here dozens of times as a kid, either with school or with my parents. Remembering the potential my young eyes saw in these monuments, the hope. Now, just a place of contentious corruption, the opposing charges on an electromagnet deadest on pulling us all into it, devouring us for its own benefit. A machine in overdrive in need of a shutdown and reboot. And me, synth hands twitching on the steering wheel, planning to somehow be a cure. Funny. Spent so long wishing to be nobody that being somebody fell in my lap.

No actual ceremony to it, but I pull up outside the brutalist, cement and glass Cap HQ, walk up to the main door and stare the surveillance cam in the lens. Smile. Big. Let them get a good look at me. "This message is for Hank Millennia. I got his message. I'm in for one more job. I've even got an idea of my own, if he's interested." I hold up a miniholo to the lens. "Ping me when you're ready to meet. I'll expect to hear from you by tomorrow, or assume that the deal is off." Cram the miniholo into the package tray beside the door, slide the drawer in until the light goes green. Package security verified. Your delivery will reach its destination in five minutes.

Stop by the Bouquet HQ as well. Building's more florid, like its tenants' words. Buttresses and filigree and parapets. Approach the surveillance cam at the front door. Drop my second miniholo in the package drawer, look at the cam. "You know who I am. After seeing what went down in the Fourth. I was there. I'm ready to take the Cap out once and for all. Get in touch if you're interested. Contact is in the miniholo." Don't even wait for the confirmation light. Turn back to the Kento, climb in, close the gullwing, speed away. It'll take an hour to get back to the Ninth. Might as well spend one last night in my apartment. Trade messages with Jozy. Hopefully there's something mindlessly distracting on the newsfeed.

twelve

Wake up to muted chimes from the pingbacks sent by Caps HQ and the Bouquet. Both willing to meet. Both open to terms. Reply with two sets of nav coordinates. A dive in the Second, and a club with private backrooms in the Fifth. "Come alone." Surprisingly, they both deign to swing by the Undercity for midday meetings.

Get up, stretch, turn on the screen. Run a quick diagnostic. Comes back all checks. Battery at 98%. Charging slower now. The Caesium pack's running down, getting hot, bad sign. Didn't last as long as advertised, but nothing does. Not going to be worth shit soon. Maybe it'll stop a bullet for me. Belly up to the kitchen counter, order a coffee from the beverage console. Black, two sugars. Sit down on the couch in front of the screen. Usual fare. Covering debates about Noncon aid, continuing cleanup in the Fourth, and some feelgood corporate nonsense about HomeCom's groundbreaking 4-shift work efficiency system. "It allows our employees to work shorter shifts, and more shifts a day so they can be more rested, and more focused and efficient in bringing folks what they need." Worse, coverage jumps to a special announcement, live from Republic Park, Ambrosia. "...truly a monumental day in the history of the Commonwealth," the reporter says, standing two hundred meters or so from the dais. "In the wake of the horrible events in the Undercity's Fourth district, Cap leader, President Hank Millennia has joined senior Bouquet party leader Alexander Beta for a joint announcement that they've promised will mark a new dawn for this city." Millennia approaches the podium with Beta at his side. "Today, after many hours of heartfelt, thoughtful debate, we come to you, the citizens of the Commonwealth, with an agreement unlike any struck in the history of this city's politics. Starting today, as we face so much division in our society, the Cap and the Bouquet will work in direct concert to develop an Undercity-wide surveillance mechanism that will ensure nothing like this disastrous fire, or the routine violence that has too long plagued those districts, ever happens again." Audience applauds. Beta steps up to the podium. "While the Bouquet and the Cap have long been divided, now is a time of solidarity. The safety of all citizens and residents of the Commonwealth is the utmost priority, and this new program will serve and protect us all, from children to elderly and all folks in between. The Bouquet will be working directly with the Cap and President Millennia to expedite this program's rollout. And our partnerships with PalCorp and HomeCom will provide us with the most-advanced technology available. Based on our calculations, this program will increase safety in the Undercity by 80% over two years. And that's something to be proud of."

Beta steps back as zecs from PalCorp and HomeCom approach to speak. Millennia and Beta shake hands beside them. Turn it off. Sick of the palaver. Amused by the unsaid. Both Millennia and Beta think they're going to be controlling the surveillance soon. Nice to get confirmation at least. Would've been a kick in the teeth to find out one side was any better than the other.

Grab my jacket, get dressed. Mosey downstairs, out to the parking tower. Jump in the Kento, just drive. Cruise out of the Ninth, up to the Loop, slide into the fast lane, push it as hard as it'll go. Everything goes vivid blur. Bright pink, purple, yellow, green. Faster and faster. Dive between Haulers, Ramblers, Dencos. Turn each into its own blur, melting into the car behind it, into the light all around. Beautiful, this place. This moment. Doesn't make me think differently about the plan. This beauty can exist with better folks at the helm, without the designed bickering and carefully-honed violence. There's just something beautiful about being lost in the blur, about the Kento, my hands on the wheel, the holos trying to keep up, the sense of place and placelessness... The Loop is living, in its own way. The living we've been taught at least. The kind where you can't stop don't stop go go fucking go. Where to? Doesn't matter. It's a circle. You'll get there if you aren't there already. And it beats the hell out of another day trapped in a living cube in the Under or a tower-floor mansion in the Over. Only thing it doesn't beat is whatever they're doing in the UC. Noncons have something figured out. People being people is way more complicated than it ever had a right to be.

Kento screen starts chiming. Don't recognize the signature. Answer it anyway. "Who's this?"

"Run, it's Jozy." Signal's a little garbled, digitized. See her on screen. Shimmer hair a vivid blue. Smiling. She's happy. Makes me happy. Funny to remember that feeling. "Mr. Spinks and I have been doing some really interesting work developing their automation systems. Can you believe the Non—the UC was doing most of their operations manually? Wild stuff. Imagine having to tell sanimechs where to clean every single day? Activating pumps and food consoles? Even the greenhouse system was still partially analog. Anyway. How's the plan going?"

"It's going. Just taking a drive right now. Clear my head," I say. "Got meetings with both of them later."

"You nervous?" she says. "You sound nervous."

"Nah. Just pessimistic. This might not work. Corps might just fill the power vacuum."

She nods. "They probably will. But they won't be ready to lead even if they start *providing services*. I've been listening in, monitoring here and there. When I'm not checking on you. The zecs are so focused on their earnings that they aren't agile enough to do anything else. Not well anyway."

"Makes me reluctant," I say. "The devil we know."

"The plan's crazy," Jozy says. "You should be reluctant. I'm just happy that you aren't blowing yourself up now. Best message I've received in a while hearing that you found a way out of *that* idea."

"Complicates the job," I say. "More to go wrong."

"That's always a thing. Upside is that more can go right. You could completely transform the Commonwealth government and erase decades of bad decisions. It's a strong bet."

Slide the Kento between two Haulers, consider trying to duck under one, slip beneath its cargo. Reconsider, lay wake and floor it again.

"I hope you're right."

"I've been right every other time since you met me," she says.

"Save for knowing about Macy Lane."

"Fuck. Yes. Okay. I dropped the ball there, but the record's still strong. And this isn't about me. This is about you trying to change the future. And I support it."

"Thanks, Joz. Fond of you."

"Fond of you, too."

"I'll be there as soon as I can," I say.

"I know you will. I'll be watching."

^^^◻

Noon. Roll up to the dive I picked in the Second. Flinty's. Crustpunk trashpub, built out of shipping containers into the side of an abandoned CommonCash subtower. Caters to digital noseringers and holospikers. Old drive-through's a fenced patio known for vapers and heavy users, light exhibitionist sexwork. Inside, each teller window's fitted with a cage and a shotgun, serving a special cocktail with a side of shut-the-fuck-up. Dance floor's basic, old. Torn up flooring, no holos, no maglifts. Just bodies mashing into one another, doing damage or taking pleasure or both. Music blasts at all hours. Place is always busy. Never many fights but the ones the loyal clientele have to finish with Over kids who come down expecting to slum. A whirling dervish of light and clattering drums and drugs and sex and denied reality. Got nothing to live for in the Under, might as well be nothing alive in here. Plus, the Over isn't even that different.

Grab a stool by the old vault door, way in the back. Best way to get someone off guard is to put them in the thick of somewhere they don't fit. Hank Millennia'll have no fans in here. This crowd isn't into his NeonCube storyline or his fights. See through him down to the rotten, self-serving core. Drag him to the back of such a situation, far from the door, far from adoration, and alone, he'll be a kitten. Or at least a limp prick. Order a neat whiskey for myself. Sit and wait.

Twenty minutes later. Flex. Millennia plods in, big trenchcoat and hat on. Terrible disguise, putting a human hulk under a few pieces of fabric and calling it concealment. Watch the door as he enters, looking for stragglers. No reason to trust him to be alone. Not stupid. Entry stays quiet as he tromps around the dance floor, hits the windows to order a drink, looks around for my pingback. Send it, make eye contact. Millennia grabs another stool, sits, sips, grits his teeth. Glares around Flinty's.

"You've got some cock on you to drag me here," he says, uncharacteristically quietly.

"You've got some on you to show up in the place that likes you the least."

Sneers. "Won't matter soon enough. The surveillance project will clean this pit and bring this whole desolate trash heap under control."

"Can't turn it off, can you?" I say. "Let's just get to business. I don't want you sweating through that trench."

"Better than getting your blood on it, synth."

"You got me there." Take a drink. Pull a smoke, light it. "Got me there... I'll do the job. I'll EMP the Bouquet offices in Ambrosia."

Millennia peers at me, slowly smiles. "I thought you were a Bouq at heart."

"Me, nah. Don't care much for being kidnapped, shutdown, but your little speech about winners really got to me," I say. "What's the point of fighting for a losing cause, dying when it's so much easier to get with the hero?"

"Bouq operatives dragged you back to their base. I smell bullshit."

"That's just Flinty's. I got caught in the middle, minding my own business. You have to understand that. Being pushed into a war you didn't start. Besides, I got out of there as soon as I could. Didn't stand and fight."

"You'd be dead if you had," Millennia says.

"I'm sure," I say. "Look. I liked your offer. I'll take the royal treatment in the Cap's Commonwealth. Prefer it over getting royally screwed in the current iteration. Even came up with a plan for it."

"Listening."

"You'll love it. Straight out of NeonCube. I told the Bouqs that I'd work for them, see. So I'm showing up there tonight to talk about and it, and boom. There goes every record, and system they have, ready for you to take control."

Millennia laughs. Chugs his drink. "I don't hate your style, synth. The old turnbuckle double cross! At least your head's on straight, and with those robot parts it's a real concern." Laughs again. Gets up. "What're you drinking? Have another with me." After I say, he stomps to the bar windows, orders another round, comes back, sits again. "You're going to love your new place, title... and fringe benefits. We take care of our own in the Cap."

"Truly psyched to be part of the team," I say, sipping. Take a drag.

"Never have to set foot in a dump like this again either." Looks at me. "Hell, maybe I'll make you head of Undercity development? Zecs are all pukes. No vision. No foresight. You've got something behind the eyes."

"Let's talk terms in a couple of days," I say. "A wise man once told me that one person can make a difference, for the right price... But now is a time for celebration." Raise my glass to his. "To the Commonwealth of the future."

Millennia taps my glass, slugs his drink. "You're my kind of people after all. Won't even talk money until after the fun part. Too many people around here begging. 'How am I supposed to live with nothing?' Figure it out, you trash asses. I did. We all did. Why should you have it easy? Suffering is its own kind of freedom."

"Let freedom ring."

Hank Millennia laughs. His wristscreen chimes. He checks it. Smiles at me. "I gotta head out, synth. But I'll be watching the newsfeed tonight for updates on the Bouq's sudden and surprise collapse with rapt anticipation. Should be historical." Millennia holds up the miniholo I left for him in an open palm, crushes it, sprinkles pieces of miniholo all over the floor between our two stools. Smiles again. Turns and walks out.

^^^o

Two hours later. Pull the Kento up to the valetmech outside Ünderclüb in the Fifth. Swankiest sex joint in the Undercity. All strobes, holos, and electrocages with bound or leathered folks inside doing what they want to do. Cigarette chicks and chads roam about taking empties, offering new drinks, meeting any needs that are, as yet, unmet. Walk in, wave off the offer to take my jacket. Accept the offer for a drink. She scans my arm to make the cover, tells me to ask for anything I might want or need. Anything. Move in slo-mo through the frame rate broken crowd, flashing bright white, falling dark, and back again over and over, endlessly. Three folks in a cage grind and writhe on one another, a petite gal with shimmer-hair set to fire walks a beefy gent on a leather leash, vape in her mouth, gag in his. Pick up murmurs as I wander through. Synth fetishes are common, still forbidden enough, still mysterious. Someone says, "You come with attachments?"

Miniholo pingback chimes as I sweep across the club. The Bouquet rep is nearby. See him. Alexander Beta in chaps, half-mask, leather vest, no shirt. Bold and so very Bouquet to go so deep undercover at Ünderclüb. Make eye contact and approach. Beta stares, sips his drink, turns away and sits on a couch shaped like a pair of lips. Follow, sit on the same couch, look straight ahead, try to look happy, flirty, like a club-goer. Beta slides closer, finally turns to me, speaks carefully, quietly into my ear.

"You left the miniholo? You worked with Harriet Alpha?" he says.

Nod. "You got it."

"I'm sure you saw the conference this morning in Republic Park. The one where the Bouquet entered into a special partnership with the Cap. You must know that while we'd gladly accept your support we cannot be directly connected."

"I'm aware of politicking and its limitations," I say.

"Good," Beta says. "I know you were involved with some of the covert affairs of my predecessor. I don't know if I approve of the tactics that were employed, but I know that I don't approve of the violent clash perpetrated by the Cap on our... private operation.

216

And for that reason alone, I authorize the continuance of the previously forwarded endeavor. However, I beg you to do everything you can to avoid any casualties that might come as a result."

"Not a problem," I say. "Plan is to hit them tonight. Building should be empty. Only the systems and records would be destroyed. Enough disarray to let you all enact emergency powers and lock them out for good."

Alexander Beta looks off wistfully. "You know, with the power of our new surveillance system, and total domain over the Commonwealth, we can build something truly wonderful. A pristine blend of corporate partnerships that will in turn design programs through which the people of the Undercity and Overcity can thrive, so long as they prove their drive and dedication. I believe that we could easily shave three or four percentage points off the poverty and suicide rates in the Undercity, and I believe we can do that in under ten years. Can you imagine? A society where everyone who's willing to work for it can be accepted and work for it, and where far fewer of them than ever before would be left behind despite their working for it?"

"Sounds like a real utopia," I say.

"Doesn't it just?" Beta continues, unironically. "Harriet Alpha dreamed of an integrated society, one where we could create enough valuable gigs to get some of the people in the Undercity up into the Overcity. But I am dreaming bigger. I see a path to near total employment, a society of strivers who, over time, influence the corps to be better. It won't be fast, but no good change ever is."

"What about this whole EMP the Cap plan?" I ask. "Isn't that going to create immediate, sweeping change?"

Beta doesn't look at me. "What you will do is a catalyzing event, one that starts the engine of change, but that engine needs fuel in the form of willing folks giving their lives to an ending they will never see. That engine needs a driver, too, which is where I and the Bouquet come in. All we can do from there is hope that the corps and the folks of the Commonwealth build something beautiful together."

"But you'll have total control. Why not just make the world better?"

Beta laughs, still not facing me. "If we did that, there'd be no need for us, and there's no need for that." Now he faces me. "The important thing, Mr. Ono-Marks, is that we fully intend to honor our

218

original agreement. Once the job is complete, wait three days, and then come visit us. I will ensure that all the arrangements are made and you can dedicate your fortune, longevity, and passion to whatever you wish. Perhaps you'll join the cause of encouraging the corps and folks of the Commonwealth to build something better?"

Bite my tongue. Certainty is a pleasure. "Sounds great," I say. "You'll be hearing from me."

"Excellent," Alexander Beta says. "It'll be a bright, new dawn for the Commonwealth."

^^^0

Three hours to showtime. Take the Kento back home to the Ninth to wait for Akari and the drop. Kill time in front of the screen. Marathon of old NeonCube episodes, happens to be showing the notorious *Death and Rebirth of Hank Millennia*. In NeonCube canon, Hank Millennia started out as Henry Century, a hungry young weakling who entered the Cube to prove his love to Estrella Star, the daughter of NeonCube's first fighter and longtime chief zec, Bobby "The Galaxy" Star. Little Henry Century bursts into the Cube just as Estrella is about to be assaulted by Teddy Jupiter, a notorious heel who had been chasing Estrella for the entire season, at first proclaiming his love for her and finally turning the unrequited advances into fuel for cartoonish levels of villainy. There had been four or five failed or bumbled previous attempts to take Estrella by force. Teddy Jupiter opened a portal in the Cube and whisked her away, but fortunately Henry Century and Doctor Dimension had already reversed its polarity, so not only was Estrella safe, but Teddy got a mouthful of fists from Henry and the Doc. Another time, Teddy convinced Estrella that she needed therapy and then, wearing a mustache and micro-monocle, tried to hypnotize her with a chronopane. Didn't work, of course, and that gave Henry and Bobby a chance to intervene and kick the crap out of him. But the *Death and Rebirth of Hank Millennia* was something special. Little Henry Century faces off against Teddy Jupiter and the Kuiper Boys. Outnumbered, and outcheated, Henry didn't stand a chance. Put up a good fight, and at the midway point in the match, it looked like he might dominate the Cube. Had Tex and Colossus Kuiper down with his brilliant signature Century Dodge. Two behemoths crashed into each other, and out cold. But then Teddy Jupiter did the unthinkable. He succeeded. Took a particle scrambler, big old cannon that takes two arms for a NeonCube fighter to lift, and six arms for anyone else, and fired on Henry until one of them hit. And it hit hard. Henry Century burst into a spray of atoms. Audience burst out in tears. Me too, back then. I was a kid. Everyone loved Henry Century. Couldn't believe he could lose, let alone be completely obliterated into absolute nothingness.

Long silence fell over the crowd. Over the whole NeonCube. Teddy Jupiter saunters over, chest puffed, and kicks at the empty space where Henry had just been, then raised his arms over his and yelled that he was champion. That he'd take his prize. Suddenly, Estrella Star, lashed to a bed, lowers down from the ceiling into the center of the Cube. Teddy's immediately all over her, professing his greatness, demanding her love, telling her she had nowhere else to turn, no one else to help her. Estrella looks all around the Cube, all around the audience. She cries for Henry, her true, now dead and departed love. Even calls for her daddy, but Bobby "The Galaxy" Star is away from the Commonwealth this week, called away by what turns out to be Teddy using a voice mod. No one to save her, Estrella tries to save herself. Rips free of the restraints and tackles Teddy. Beats him up pretty good too, has him on the ropes when those Kuiper Boys come to and make the odds impossible. With Tex on one arm, and Colossus on the other, Teddy Jupiter's "prize" is stuck and ready and seized. Teddy crawls on top of her, starts kissing her, despite her protests. Crowd turns on him immediately. Hisses and boos. Throwing drinks and even Teddy Jupiter merch. All of it bounces off the field covering the Cube.

That's when it happens. The impossible. The amazing. The truly miraculous. Henry Century returns, bigger, stronger, with a huge beard. A laser lowers from the ceiling, shoots beams in a fast grid, as if printing him anew from the beyond. When the crowd realizes what's happening the boos turn to cheers. "Kill them, Henry!" they yell. And this renewed hulk pops his jaw, flexes, and calls out to the crowd. "Henry Century is dead. Now is the dawn of a new millennia. A Hank Millennia!" Hank Millennia breaks the Kuiper Boys in minutes, lifts Tex overhead, slams him into Colossus, ties the duo in knots and kicks them around the Cube like a football. Turns his attention to Teddy Jupiter, who cowers the way a heel should. Millennia pounds on Teddy for what feels like hours, then throws him into the air in the middle of the Cube, climbs up the outer wall of the Cube and divebombs him into the floor all before Teddy could hit the ground. Teeth go flying. The crowd roars. Hank Millennia holds Teddy up by his hair, says, "Our beef ends now. You're never coming back to the NeonCube because now this is Hank Millennia's domain!" Unties Estrella Star and they kiss, then Millennia lifts her up, carries her out of the Cube, out of the arena. Next anyone sees of them, it's a camfeed on the Cube's screen showing them set up in a swanky hotel room.

One of my favorite episodes of the NeonCube. It's classic in every way. Used to feel like a story of redemption, of Good triumphing over Evil. Too bad that Millennia took the fame he got in the Cube and turned it into a narrative of individual might makes right. Fifteen years later, he's ready to destroy half the Commonwealth to keep control, prove something to himself. Even watching now leaves a bad taste. Not the same. Nothing ever is. Reality has a way of disarming mythology, if we're willing to study at it closely, eyes and ears open.

Door chimes. Check the surveillance cam. Akari. Right on time. Follow her out to the parking column. Her Hauler's parked beside the Kento. Smiles as she approaches the gate doors of the big van, pops them open, flicks on the compartment light, turns and looks at me expectantly. Inside, there are two synth bodies that look exactly like me, down to the slight asymmetry of my nose and eyes.

"Well?" she says.

"They're great. It's creepy how great they are."

"Right!?" Akari says. "And you thought I couldn't duplicate you."

Nod. "I was wrong," I say. "Let's see how they work."

Akari climbs into the back of the Hauler, opens the torso panels on each, taps away at the operational screens. Synths boot up, gasp for air performatively, sit up and look at us.

"Greetings, I am Run Ono-Marks," they say, slightly staggered, in my voice. "Please provide task input."

Akari looks at me. "Let me show you something," she says. Taps away at the screens again. "This is the balance and grace test task."

Both synths climb to their feet, turn to each other, bow, and then start dancing like it's some kind of Eighteenth Century cotillion. They mirror each other, move with precise fluidity, spin, hop, bob and twirl.

"Now, execute pattern two," Akari says.

The synths stop, mid-motion, reset and start breaking, popping and locking, windmilling and headspinning. Starts to make me dizzy to look at it.

"Great stuff," I say. "Too bad we don't have a competition coming up."

Akari laughs. "Just wanted to demo their dexterity. Here's the real stuff." She taps away at the torso screens again. "This is Task Run New Future." Akari taps again to confirm and steps back.

The two of me suddenly and creepily take on my exact posture and resting stance. "Ready when you are, chief," they say. "Looking forward to changing the world." Then they both take out smokes, light them with their fingertip fires, and take a drag.

Never realized how cartoonishly film noir I was until just this moment. "Not sure if I should be insulted or impressed," I say.

"Why not both?" Akari says, smirking.

"Thanks for these."

"Sure, sure. One thing you have to remember, they have a somewhat limited range, so you'll have to enter the command pretty much right nearby where they're supposed to execute. Then just point them in the right direction. Sorry it's not better."

225

Shake my head. "Don't be. This is better if there's a little risk for me. Makes it real. And besides, it took you a few hours. You're a genius."

"Save the praise, Run," Akari says. "Just hold up your end and get me out of here when it's done."

Nod. "You have my word."

The two synths parrot me, "You have my word."

"Let's turn them off now," I say.

Akari shuts them down, runs through the procedure for booting and activating the program with me a couple of times to make sure I've got it down. Then I pop the hatchback and load them into the back of the Kento, curled up in each other like a couple of yins without any yangs.

"They'll stay inert until you activate them, but after that the EMP could be a bit... unstable," Akari says. "So it's best to wind these two up and send them straight at the targets. You don't want to be caught up in the resonance wave. I don't think I have to tell you why."

"You mean because it would mean the total cessation of the synth organs that keep my fragile human brain alive?" I say.

Akari touches her nose. "Just be careful."

"I will. Now get out of here. Go put on the newsfeed. You might see me."

Akari throws me a salute, turns, jumps into her Hauler, drives away.

Pull out a smoke, light it, stare out at the Undercity sprawling all around. Wonder what it'll look like in a few weeks, months, years. Hope that it's better than this. It'd pretty much have to be.

thirteen

Zero hour. Eight-thirty PM. With two synths of me in back, take the Kento through the Ninth to the Loop, speed along the pink and blue glowing highway lined with holos up to the Overcity, and exit at Ambrosia. Streets are teeming with well-to-dos, zecs and gov staff wandering about, suited, talking close and quiet. Lots of normal folks too, Overcity normal, high-fashion types, tourists checking out the seat of leadership, parents showing their children the shiny wrapper that covers the sausage, young lovers kissing on benches, waiting in line at clubs and bars, vying for theatre tickets. Holos and corp security hover about, doing the same amount of passive advertising. A few people let their dogs and other exotic or cloned pets off leash at Republic Park, letting them frolick among the public grasses, piss on the statues, and spring into the background of pics families try to take.

Be interesting to see what the world is like for these folks after it's done. Will it even change? Probably all far enough removed from the fault lines in the Commonwealth that even a seismic shift couldn't shake them, upend their realities. Not right away. Once they felt some discomfort, the discomfort of disorder, they'd be blessed with awareness. And they'd build something better. Almost anything would be better at this point. All they have to do is look to the Noncons, the UC, and take notes. Better is pre-chewed, pre-written. Unless they all choose to run away from it. Can't fixate on that now. Prime the canvas first, then worry about mixing paints.

Circle the Park a few times, get a lay of the land. No checkpoints or extra security. Parking towers for each headquarters and the Assembly are emptied out. Workers've gone home for the day, buildings ought to be abandoned. Makes the procedure quick enough. Each synth approaches the main entrances, cuts open the main door with the laser tip to their index fingers, sidles inside calmly to the center of the building, engages the EMP reaction, leading a massive, resonant electromagnetic pulse to surge through the entire structure knocking out and wiping the data from every computer system in the radius. Buildings will just be husks of a failed experiment. Take months for the corps to put anything back together, independently, and in that time, the rudderless Commonwealth will have let down enough people, from benefit recipients to zecs with contracts. Blame will fly in all directions, and folks'll have the chance to decide what they want for tomorrow. The exciting bit, both synths have a shielded black box that contains POV of my convos with each party. The Bouquet black box will tell how the Cap wanted to take control. The Cap black box will show how the Bouquet was willing to do anything it took to rule with a smile and a fist. The truth will be out, their cowardly games revealed. Newsfeeds'll eat that shit right up.

Folks will too. They'd better.

Pull over on Paramount Circle, put the Kento in park, pop the gullwing and climb out. Open the hatchback and sit both of the synths up. Open their chest screens, enter the commands to bring them to life. Each other me sits up, attentive and ready. Asks for orders. Tell them to pile into the backseat of the Kento, hold tight. Close the hatch, hop back into the driver's seat, take another lap quick lap with the Kento.

Funny having duplicates, triplicates of yourself. Start wondering if the weird little ticks the synths have, one chewing on the inside of its cheek, the other absent-mindedly scratching its neck over and over, are my own or something Akari made up. Not much self to be aware of now, just the neck up, but the synths put everything in italic bold. Imagine rolling into a fight with two more of me? Or hitting a club as triplets? Should've thought of the fun in life earlier. Wouldn't have extracted me from the abject poverty of gigwork, but maybe I'd see the city differently. Or not. Advantage of a synth body. Put everything through the brain. See it for what it is, not for representation or easy manipulation or catchiness. Of course, doesn't undo memory. Only thing that makes us truly human and alive. I was a child once. Remember it. Likely always will. That means pretty much everything. And nothing at all.

One synth chats the other up on the topic of industrial design. Not my topic space. The other talks about Akari. How smart she is. How capable. How cute. Funny what we learn from people through the things and lives they create.

"You boys ready for the big show?" I ask them via the rearview.

Both synths stop conversing, perk up, process my question.

"No commands matched. Please restate command," they say in unison.

"Never mind," I say. "Just keep being pretty."

Weave the Kento through the evening traffic, pull into the Republic Park promenade. Wave to the LykTek rentals doing security. One eats a sandwich while the others chuckle. Pull up to the steps at the Bouquet offices first, twist back in my seat, tap on the screen to start the process. Timer appears, fifteen minutes. Tap again to start the clock, then order the synth out of the car. Confirms. Clockwork me climbs out of the Kento on the passenger side, saunters up the steps toward the building, raises its hands to mimic taking a pic, then starts laser carving at the big glass doors. Programming means this me cuts a bit, steps back and motions like they're taking another pic, then back to it. A skill long honed by graffiti artists, now applied to ending decades of destructive infighting and greedy listlessness.

Me and the other me take the Kento over to the Cap headquarters on the opposite end of Republic Park. The daunting cement and glass structure looms here, the way death might over a cathedral. Turn around and tap at the chest screen for the remaining me, start the program, pop the passenger side gullwing. Flip my hood, climb out of the car, help the synth out of the backseat. It starts for the huge, glass double doors. I sit on the hood of the Kento, take out a smoke, light it. Look up at the building. Just a few days ago they had me. Lane had duped me. Millennia nearly killed me. Killed a whole mess of Bouqs instead, all in secret, all for the power. I'd've been dumped, processed by a sanimech, spilled out the pipe into the Wastes to slowly dissolve among irradiated toxins until I was spread across the landscape on the wind.

"You've got a lot on your shoulders," I say to my copy.

The synth stops, turns and looks at me. "It is also your shoulders."

Nod. "Feels that way. Never was big on revenge."

"Revenge is just forgiveness with mutually-assured destruction," the remaining me says.

Makes you think. "Where'd you come up with that?" I ask.

"It is in my programming based on Akari's understanding of you."

"She thinks I'm pretty smart."

"Perhaps we are," it says.

The synth plods up the steps to the Cap offices, starts pulling the same tricks, take a pic, step up, start lasering, take another pic, repeat. Through the narrow windows, see movement. No folks should be in there. Something's wrong. Run up the steps to my copy, still working, peer around it. Two figures sitting in the first floor boardroom, one hulking, one smaller, a plume of smoke rises from the big one. Shit. Use the advanced vision specs in the hood to get a closer look. Shit. Hank Millennia and Macy Lane, meeting up again. The EMP won't kill them, but they'll sure know who I am when they see my duplicate come walking in, right by their windows. No time to reprogram the synth. No way to stop the process now. Check my charge. Sitting at 44%. The Caesium pack's all but dead, still trying to charge, not getting anywhere. Only option is going to cost me what I've got left. Without it the Cap will be the only sitting party and the Commonwealth'll be no better off than it is now. Worse.

"Pause program," I say, and synth me acknowledges.

Open my forearm panel, unlock my chest compartment, pull out my incog unit, the auxiliary power source, slap the compartment closed. Check status again. Charge down to 18%. Drops to 17% then 16% as the system calibrates, tries to read the Caesium pack and the drain on the primary. Pop the chest compartment on the synth me, install the incog and the aux source, tap at its chest screen, set the incog to PalCorp maintenance worker. Just like that, this synth me turns into a corp handyman, jumpsuit, name badge and all. Step back, check the seams. Looks good. "Continue program," I say. Synth looks at me, with its incog face, no longer me. "Acknowledged." Continues cutting the door open.

Leave the synth and sprint toward the windows of the boardroom. See Millennia and Lane inside, laughing, thick. Whatever deal they're making won't be good for anyone but them, and possibly not even for both. Just have to keep them in the room, not looking in the lobby, not checking the front door. Get around to the side, farthest from the door as I can manage and still be noticed. Press my face up against the window, start slapping at the pane, really hammering it. Nothing. Must be aural shielded. Keeps prying ears out and negates distractions from tourists or protestors. Flip my fingertip laser open and start boring into it. Just a small hole. Enough to get sound through. Charge warning chimes. 10%. Just need enough to get back to the Kento, get out of range. Timer gives me six more minutes. Monitor on my arm screen shows the synth me already deep inside the Bouquet. Other me is about to break through the front of the Cap. Laser pops through the boardroom window, pull my pistol from my hip, set it to silent, and aim for the hole. Just trying to hit something loud, like a vase sitting on a credenza along the wall. Line up the shot, pull the trigger. Still got it. Shot threads the needle, obliterates the vase, shards flying everywhere. Millennia and Lane jump, turn to look, see the shattered vase. Millennia runs toward the window, Lane dives to the floor.

Take another shot, quickly, at Millennia's knee. Got to get him down, can't let him leave that room, muck up the works. The beefy former champion sidesteps my shot, growls, keeps charging the window. Can't tell if he knows it's me or if he just knows someone messing with him is about to get it. Set my iron for incap, have to press the barrel right against the opening to avoid losing everything from the spread. Pop off one round, surge of energy pulses out in a cone, smacks Millennia square in the chest. Old man slows down, stumbles, falls to one knee, a lot like when Henry Century lost that match. He breathes heavy, sees my face, sneers. Uses what's left of his consciousness to let me know with a finger across his throat that this isn't over. Probably isn't. Millennia slides down to the floor. Nighty night. Get to wake up to a changed world. Wonder how your winning attitude will hold up if there's no more war, just a chance to start over. Lane peeks up, she's under the table like her dealings, catches my face. Sense that recognition. Think about waving, think better of it, just smirk, shake my head, back away from the window.

Timer chimes. Two minutes. Charge meter alert chimes. 6% left. Cutting it close. Sprint back to the Kento. Close the gullwings, start it up. Tear out of Republic Park just as the first EMP goes, a brilliant sphere of iridescent purple and green light blossoms inside the Bouquet. Kento can't move fast enough. The pulse laps at it, shuts the systems down, start slowing down. Then the EMP in the Cap lights up. Another sphere springs out, crafting a Venn diagram with the first. Two huge EMP waves combine, swirl and bathe everything in purple and green. Quite a sight. Blast engulfs the whole park, the Kento, and me. Weird feeling, sudden complete scramble and shutdown. Don't know where I am, or who, just feel tired. Seat's pretty cozy, warm, crazy glow outside must be some kind of storm. Best to just hunker down for a bit, rest my eyes, wait for the weather to cha

fourteen

"**H**ello? Can you hear me?" a voice says. "Never worked on a synth before. Where's your status pane?"

Can't move. Can't see. Can't speak.

"Oh fuck it," another voice says. "Shock him. There's no more time to waste looking for an instruction manual."

Two points of pressure on my chest. A blast of energy. Something starts working. Bright light in my eyes. Can't see beyond it. Eyes adjust slowly. Darkness fades into flashing lights, dark blue sky, flicker of holos. Lots of folks stomping all around. PalCorp guards, medics. Have a hard time focusing. Where am

I? On the ground? Grass? A car sits silent beside me. Blink again and again. Mouth is dry, sticky. Two shadows loom over me. Can almost make out a face.

"What... what happened?" I say. "Who are you?"

"You're awake?" the medic says. "Holy crap." Medic turns and yells over her shoulder. "Stan! Come here!" She turns back to me. "Don't know how you survived it. Some kind of attack, it took out all the electronics in the area. I'm a medic... Sara." She taps the nametag on her white PalCorp Medical jumpsuit. "I don't know how you—"

Another form shows up, kneels over me. Must be this Stan.

"Amazing," he says to Sara. "Excellent work. It's nice to know we could save one." He looks at me. "You're quite the specimen. You don't have a lot of charge left. Only two percent. So we need to load you into a Hauler and get you to your preferred maintenance facility. Do you consent to that?"

Nod. "Did someone die here? She said there was an explosion."

"You don't remember?" Stan says. "Interesting." He turns to Sara. "Sara, let's get intake done on this one and get them loaded up." Stan walks away, his jumpsuit bathed in flickering blue and red light.

Sara kneels down again. "So, what's your name?"

Name? Must have one. What is it...? "I don't know," I say.

"This Kento here claims it belongs to a Run Ono-Marks. Does that sound familiar to you at all?"

Think for a moment. Try to remember. Shake my head. "Maybe? I don't... I'm sorry."

"That's okay," she says. "Nothing to worry about. Temporary loss of memory is normal for concussions." She takes out a handscreen and starts tapping at it. "Do you recall how you got here? What you were doing when the explosion went off?"

Nothing. There's nothing in my head. "I don't know. I can't remember anything. Please, tell me what happened."

Sara smiles and nods. "Well, like I said, there was an explosion. An electromagnetic pulse. That kind of explosion can do very serious damage to tech or a synth like you. You're lucky to be alive. Let's get you into a Hauler and get you charged. I bet you'll feel a whole bunch better after that."

"But, someone died?" I say. "Who would do this?"

Sara looks down. "The President... was killed in the blast inside the Cap Party offices. His synth heart shutdown and we couldn't get to him fast enough."

241

The President? Something terrible has happened. "How did I survive if... if he didn't?"

"I'm not sure, but my best guess is that the nanites in your synth body came back online quickly enough that they could start repairing your organs to put you in a kind of standby mode," Sara says. Her handscreen chimes. She looks down, reads. "Okay, I have confirmation that you're probably the Run Ono-Marks who owns this Kento here." Holds up the screen. There's a photo of a face. "Looks a lot like you, I think. Let's get you into the Hauler. Since this is your first ride with PalCorp Medical the trip is free. Oh, and we'll hook your car up and take you to... Hmm. Akari's Technophilia in the Seventh. Does that sound right to you, Run?"

"I'm just going to have to trust you, Sara," I say.

She stands up, waves a couple more medics over. Slide a gurney under me, activate the hoverfield, guide me toward a Hauler. Sky overhead almost has stars. Beautiful night really. Load me into the Hauler's box. Sara climbs in after me. Thanks the other two medics. Tells them to hook up the car. My car. She clambers about the ambulance, digs through a compartment, emerges with a connector. Holds it up to my chest, eyeballs it, plugs it in.

"Okay, I'm going to turn on our portable charger now. I'll warn you that it's not great, but it'll keep you from shutting down on the trip. Is that okay?"

"Yeah. Thanks," I say. "Where am I?"

"Right now?" she says, fiddling with a screen embedded in a console in back of the Hauler. "We're in Republic Park, the home of government in the Commonwealth. That's the megacity you're in. This is the Overcity, and where we're going is the Undercity."

"Undercity?"

She chuckles. "It's not a good name. Too many negative implications if you ask me."

"Do I live there?" I say. "In the Undercity."

Sara looks down at her handscreen again. "Hmm. It looks like you might. I can't tell exactly where without verifying your Cash account. Do you want to do that?"

Shake my head. "That's okay. Hopefully it'll come back to me."

"Nobody likes the fees," she says. "Okay. This shouldn't hurt, but it might. I really don't know synth maintenance. I'm sorry."

Dials up the portable charger. Feel hot around the connection, warm everywhere else. Hum of the device is pleasant, almost relaxing. Vision comes into focus.

Fog on my mind starts to lift. Flashes of my life. A woman with shimmer-hair. Driving that Kento. Parents and an incredible sadness.

Sara hovers over me, taps at the screen in my chest. "Your diagnostics say they're all good. That's probably positive, right? Looks like you're up to 4% already. Now, why don't you relax and watch the newsfeed for a bit while we drive. Try to stay still. We'll get you to Akari's as soon as we possibly can." She smiles, pulls a rumbleseat out from a compartment in the Hauler, sits and buckles herself in. Then taps at her handscreen and the back door of the Hauler turns into a giant holoscreen. Newsfeedcaster appears on screen, somber-faced.

"Tragedy tonight in Ambrosia as two electromagnetic pulse explosions kill President Hank Millennia and, disable and erase generations of Cap and Bouquet Party data and programming. Former child prodigy Macy Lane was also affected by the blast. More on their statuses as details become clear.▢

"Corporate security and medical is on scene now, with PalCorp leading a multi-company effort to investigate the event. And all members of the Cap and Bouquet parties are currently under corporate lockdown with additional skilled security to ensure no one else is harmed. What exactly happened here? Was it an attack? And if so, what motivated such a dramatic and destructive assault on our government? Heather Mead reports." Camera changes to feed from Republic Park.◙

"Thank you, David. Truly a tragic day for the Commonwealth. President Hank Millennia is dead in an EMP blast that stopped his synth heart. Millennia received the replacement heart following years of steroid abuse during his tenure in the NeonCube. Alexandre Beta of the Bouquet has interim presidential powers, however we're unlikely to see him or any other government officials until corporate forces can confirm the danger has passed.◙

"The attack does appear to have been coordinated. We're hearing initial reports from PalCorp and LyfTek officials that a pair of black boxes have been recovered from the scene, and we're hopeful that those will shed some light on today's events."◙

Camera switches back to the newsfeeddesk. "Were there any other injuries from the attack, Heather?"◉

"Well, David, we've been told that two other folks were harmed by the blast. One, a local whose identity is locked behind PalCorp Medical's privacy firewall, was driving around the loop at Republic Park when the incident occurred. The other is Commonwealth child success story Macy Lane. We've been told she is stable, but that the blast may have damaged positronic brain mods she had installed and so far the medics are unclear on the lasting damage."◉

"Horrible. Just horrible, Heather," David says. "Can you give us a sense of the scene? How are the folks of Ambrosia reacting to this incident? How would you assess the corporate response?"◉

Heather Mead nods. "The scene is relatively calm at present, David. PalCorp and LyfTek are maintaining a barrier around Republic Park. HomeCom and CommonCash are reportedly sending their own teams to provide additional support. The folks here in

Ambrosia are gathering at the perimeter, looking on. There are a lot of confused faces out here tonight, but PalCorp executives assure us that details are forthcoming. We want to remind viewers that the Commonwealth's core operations remain automated, and to remain calm while all of us try to put the pieces together of today's tragic and surprising events."▪

Turn away from the newsfeed and look out the window. Hauler winds through and out of Ambrosia. Folks in the streets, huddling together, staring up at the holos projecting the news. Corporate security just milling around, directing traffic, ushering folks to go about their business, go do whatever they were planning to. Cut through Elysium, Avalon, Eden and Tian. Story's pretty much the same. Folks looking surprised, scared, but not daunted. Clubs still bumping, bars still full, stores and towers still bustling. As the Hauler is queuing to pull into the Loop toward the Undercity, see two LyfTek guards push a woman from Eden back. Woman starts screaming at them. Can't hear it, but can see it. Guard pulls a static club and whacks her with it. She hits the ground in a heap. Crowd goes nuts. Riot starts.

Hundred or two some folks surround the guards, start yelling and pummeling, then flood into the street. Hauler shakes and makes a sudden maneuver, turns sharply, barrels down some sidestreet.

See it again and again. Corporate guards taking their crowd control gig too seriously, folks in the Overcity pushing back. We wind back past the same holosigns as before, Tian, Elysium, Avalon. Wouldn't call it chaos out there, just confusion. But the kind of confusion that no one wants to be in the middle of. Still, it doesn't seem to reach everywhere. Plenty of streets are calm, but the ones that aren't, really aren't.

Sara sits uncomfortably in the rumble seat. "Don't worry. We'll get you where you need to go."

Look back at her. "I'm not worried. You shouldn't be either. Nobody seems to be mad at medics."

She squirms in her seat, but smiles anyway.

Hauler makes its way into the Loop, cuts down into the Undercity. In these streets it looks like a party. Folks dancing in the streets, kids running around wild, a couple of teens smacking a Cap logo holo back and forth with a pair of conduit pipes. No corporate presence at all down here. Just revelry.

Wonder why. Sometimes folks take the same news in different ways, I suppose.

Sara turns up the newsfeed as the Hauler winds through dark, Undercity streets.

"Breaking news from the Republic Park attacks," David says. "Heather, tell us what you've just uncovered."◘

"Thanks, David," she says. "I have an exciting update from the recovered black boxes found at the scene of today's EMP blasts. Our embedded LyfTek reporter has just uploaded the contents of those black boxes to NewsServer One. A warning as we have not yet viewed this record, and we cannot vouch for the appropriateness of the content."◘

Both black boxes play, connecting the Cap, Hank Millennia, the Bouquet, Alexandre Beta, and every corporation to dueling conspiracies intent on seizing total control of the Commonwealth. It covers their work to undermine the Noncons. It shows their plans for turning the Undercity into a kind of penal colony. And all of it comes straight from their own mouths.◘

For a second, I feel like I might remember some of it. Just can't be sure. Feels like I was there?

After the footage, Heather Mead reappears on screen, visibly shaken. "David, I can't even begin to describe what we've just seen, but I believe it might be evidence that both the Cap and the Bouquet intended to destroy the other to take over the Commonwealth." She shakes her head. "And that their corporate partners were at least tangentially culpable." She looks away from the cam lens. "Can we verify this? It's definitely real? Holy fu-"

The cam shuts off. Screen's black for a moment. Then back on the newsfeeddesk. "Apologies for our technical difficulties there. It appears that the Commonwealth may well have been attacked from the inside. It's difficult, if not impossible, to refute the footage you've just seen and will likely see many more times over the next few weeks. The idea that our leadership in the Cap and the Bouquet would plot against each other and against this great city was once unthinkable and now laid bare. That the corporations, long the third arm of our governance, a stopgap against tomfoolery, would also be involved is an alarming blight on the Commonwealth, its ideals, and most importantly, its people.▪

"We will continue to follow this story as it develops. And we request, for the safety of everyone in the Commonwealth, that folks remain calm."▪

Interesting. A trickle of memories, but nothing substantial. What's happening out there is big, obviously. Read the room. But doesn't hit me like a ton of bricks. Wish I could remember anything clearly.

Hauler stops, lurches. Sara unbuckles and rises from her rumble seat, steps carefully over to me, looking sick. "Looks... looks like you're at 12% now. I'm sure your usual maintenance person can take care of the rest."

"Thank you," I say. "Are you alright?"

"The whole society is crumbling around us," she says. "I don't think I am."

"You know you're one of the good ones, right?" I say. "Folks might be upset, but they usually know where to put it. They probably won't mess with you."

"Probably," she says.

"Listen to what that David guy says," I say. "What's going on seems like it had to come to light, and we'll all be better off for knowing it."

"They do say that the truth hurts, don't they?" she says.

Nod. "If you've got to be hurt by something, might as well be that."

Sara disconnects the charging cable from my chest, back door of the Hauler opens. Two medics from before hustle in, grab the gurney, activate the hoverfield, usher me out. They push me toward the door of a small shop, no signage. A woman stands at the door, sees me. Yells, "Run!" and sprints over, pulling me inside. The big medics disconnect the Kento from the Hauler, push it over to a parking spot in a lot behind this little shop, climb back in. Watch the woman who knows my name run up to Sara, nod a few times, embrace her. Sara gets back in the Hauler, and it speeds away through the dark, neon-lit streets. Woman who knows my name pushes me inside the building, looks me straight in the eye, cocks her head.

"Alright, Run," she says. "Looks like you did it. Let's get you patched up."

Fifteen

A void. Just a void. Pure, inky blackness interrupted by nothing. Warm, soft inky blackness. Like being wrapped in a blanket, hurtled through space. Comfort in the expanse. Flashes of light, shapes, splashes of lightning turning into memories. Here I am at the entrance of the Commonwealth Zoo, holding my mother's hand. The smell of animals, so strange and unique, so pure and welcoming. Mother tousles my hair, tells me I can go wherever I want, just stay close. Running down the paths, past the giraffes, polar bears, mammoths, toward the dinosaurs. Anything was possible. Here I am at the hospital, standing at the counter with the nurse assigned to me, hearing the news the first time, not comprehending it. This must be a dream. The dream to end them all. And it did. Falling to my knees, burying my face in my hands. Crying to steal the scant moments of relief in between the gasps for air. Here I am at the old Commonwealth synth warehouse, signing the paperwork to sell my heart, my liver, my lungs for C200,000 each, not knowing how cheap that was, not knowing that my problems wouldn't go away with more sacrifice. Laying on the table as they activate the neural interrupter, temporarily deactivate my nerves and cut me open. Wide awake the whole time. Lasers melting flesh, grumbling surgeons, the popping feeling when the skin's elasticity gives way and peels open. Seeing my own heart there, in another man's hands, slipped into a preservation cube for easy transport and sale. Here I am outside Akari's just a few days ago, hearing a shadowy figure offer me something I couldn't refuse, choosing the call, not knowing what the call really was. Here I am sleeping with Jozy Jinx in her big apartment in Avalon, not knowing whether to trust her or trust myself. Here I am in Hank Millennia's office, taking a beating. Here I am in the Wastes, discarding my delusions, the lies I'd been told, seeing a group of folks living together for each other. Here I am in Republic Park urging the Kento to go faster, trying to escape radiant waves of EMP, knowing that I'm about to eat shit and probably die. Here I am back in the UC, with Jozy, trying to live quietly, simply, trading good deeds for good deeds, giving of myself and getting something meaningful in return. Here I am getting into bed at the end of a long day, Jozy already asleep beside me, the churning purple and orange and blue storming skies outside the window taking all my restlessness from me, leaving me with sweet, restful calm.

And then a furry little creature, a chinchilla, the Chinchilla bounds from the darkness up onto the bed and climbs onto my chest, smiling at me, its rodentine chompers glistening with the irradiated tumult outside, its eyes gentle and kind.

"Look at you," it says. "Look at you."

"Only so much I can see, being that I'm me."

"You see more than you think. Much more. Look at me," the Chinchilla says. "I am everything and nothing. It's difficult work, but someone has to do it."

The Chinchilla's face slides down its body, to its belly, then pushes through its back out to the tip of its tail. It flicks at me, laughing from the tail's tip, and then the face melts back into it, and pops out where it would normally be.

"Does that hurt?" I ask.

The Chinchilla shakes its whole body, its soft fur slowing down so much that I can see each bristle rustle like a blade of grass, a field from some story about wide open spaces. "I cannot hurt. I can only continue," it says.

"But, when does it end?" I ask.

"It doesn't. You don't. There simply isn't."

"Then what's the point?" I ask. "What does it mean?"

"You've already sorted that out," the Chinchilla says. "You just don't know what questions to ask yourself."

"But what if it's too hard, what's next? What if I can't—"

The Chinchilla burrows into my neck, pressing its delicate plushness into the flesh I have left. "When it's hard, you must soften," it says. "Reshape. Become anew. The things that are immovable will not respond to force. They will not respond at all. But you will."

The creature melts into me. I feel it tumbling, somersaulting throughout my body. It's gentle and curious, moving things around, making paths, reorganizing everything. A soft alien visitor exploring whatever form there is that is mine among all the infinite void. Watch as it finds my head and rolls around with my thoughts, bathing in them, tossing them out of order, letting them fall into a chaotic pile that somehow feels more ordered and natural than I can remember. There is sense in the disorder, knowledge in the unlearning. The Chinchilla weaves its way back to my chest, emerges, grasps my jaw with its tiny hands.

"Be soft," it says. "Soft enough that nothing contains you. But, never so soft that you'd make a good coat."

It nuzzles its nose against mine and slowly fades away into the void as a pinpoint of light pierces, expands, and blinds.

Come to in Akari's shop on her charging table. Something feels different, wrong. Look down at my hands, legs. They aren't the same. What'd she do? Eyes adjusting to the light, can't make out much. Ears flooded with the sound of rushing water. Synth heart racing. Then she takes my hand.

"Stay calm, Run," she says. "And don't be mad."

"Mad?" I say, my voice raspy.

Akari leans over me, sheepish. "I might've decided to give you an upgrade without your permission. The good news is, it seems like it worked. The PerpetMot generator is humming along."

"PerpetMot? Where'd you get that?"

She smirks. "Fell off a truck," she says.

"I see."

"Well, to be more accurate, the Hauler that normally delivers repair parts had some of last year's parts taking up space, so I offered to store it for them for free. They probably won't even remember, with everything happening out there. And if they do, I'll be long gone. Right?"

"What's happening out there?" I say. "Last thing I remember is trying to get away from the EMP blast."

Akari grins. "You're lucky you remember anything at all. Your pathways were fried when you got here. After I installed the generator and switched out your other components, I did a little remapping. Glad to know that I didn't screw it up."

Bite my lip. "Probably wouldn't remember if you did, would I?"

"Well, there's that." She winks. "A lot's happened in three days. Chaos out there. The folks in the Overcity have been setting up anti-corp zones all over the place, pushing PalCorp and LyfTek and HomeCom, all of them, off the streets and out of the towers. Newsfeed's only talking about those black boxes, the criss cross plots by the Bouqs and Caps, the corp zecs backing the deals in exchange for more control."

"Three days?"

"I'm good at synth engineering, Run, but I'm not good enough to do it in an evening."

"Wasn't being critical, just surprised to be out of commission that long," I say.

Akari nods. "Yeah. You missed all the partying down here. Now things are getting a little gritty in the Under. I don't think it's going to be safe down here much longer. Punks and angry corp deserters think they get run of the place while the cats are away."

"But is it better now?" I ask. "Better for what I did?"

She disconnects me from the charging table, helps me sit up. "I think it will be. Gotta have Winter before the Spring."

Nod. Check out my new body. The PerpetMot parts are shiny, have built in incog. Check my forearm screen, run a diagnostic. Comes back all checks. Nanites are advanced, at the ready. Hand tools and foot add-ons are precision honed. Even have a built in aural disruptor. Charge meter reads N/A. No more status bar, just a turning gear, bright green, with OK stamped underneath. Pop my thigh compartment, gun's inside. Swing my legs over the table, hop down, stretch. No more grinding or wear. Joints are top notch. Feel more limber than before, simultaneously coiled like a snake, ready to strike. Finally seems like being a synth is better than having a human body, or least the upsides outweigh the down.

"Anything I need to know about the new set up?" I ask.

"Ooh. Yes. I was hoping you'd ask," she says. "It's thirty percent lighter, so you'll probably have to get used to that when running, jumping, that sort of thing. Everything else is about the same, just top of the line."

"I saw on the diagnostic," I say. "Thanks for this."

"One more thing," she says. "It has a programmable rest mode. Your old battery and auxiliary had an adaptable cycle. Designers trying to mimic circadian rhythms. But the folks at PerpetMot let you set your own, so if you're a night owl you can rest during the day, that sort of thing. You'll figure it out, but it's in settings under 'time adaptability'.

And... you're welcome. It's the least I could do, really. I just can't wait to get out of he—"

Loud pounding on the door to the clinic. Akari runs to the surveillance screen.

"Fuck. There's a group of PalCorp soldiers out there."

Rush to the screen and take a look. Recognize a couple of them. They were cleaning out the orphanage when all this started.

"Get your stuff packed," I tell her. "I'll be right back."

"You're going out there?" she says.

"Why not? Feel like I could live forever."

Open the clinic door. See a huddle of six PalCorp troops, stroking their rifles, looking pissed and entitled.

"Can I help you boys?"

"Get out of the way, and we don't have to hurt you," the Leader says. "We just want to take a look at your equipment, maybe requisition some of it for ourselves. You understand. The world's not as safe as it used to be."

"Plenty safe in here," I say. "Maybe you could leave your weapons outside?"

The Leader laughs. Other PalCorp guys follow suit.

"So there's no chance you'll just walk away, then?" I say.

Leader grits his teeth. "Barely a chance that you will at this rate, synth."

No other choice. Power kick the Leader square in the chest, send him flying backward, knocking two of the others down with his weight. Duck and spin, tripping another guard, while drawing the pistol from my leg and pulling Akari's door shut behind me with my other hand. Set the iron to shock, turn and fire off one round into the tripped guard. He falls limp, drops his rifle. Jump over the Leader and guards he fell into, throw a left hook into the neck of one standing guard, a roundhouse into the jaw of the other. Both start falling. Fire off two more shock shots, put them to sleep before they hit the ground. Remaining two guards and the Leader climb to their feet, fire off a few rounds. Can't be hit. The new body's too fast, too agile. Grab one rifle by the barrel, use my other arm as a fulcrum, smack the PalCorp chump in the chin with butt of his own gun. Take quick aim at the other, fire a shock shot into his right leg. Starts collapsing, drops his weapon, extends his arm to catch himself. Take another shot, zap that arm, it goes limp, buckles like Udon under him, splats hard on the pavement, tooth soars into the air. Leader holds his rifle on me, hands shaking like crazy, barrel wobbling up and down and side and side.

"I'll fucking kill you, synth," he says, finger fondling the trigger.

"I doubt that." Lunge to side, duck, kick his legs out from under him, catch him. I take the rifle from his hands, toss it into the street. Smile. Pop him in the mouth with a balled fist.

Leader groans, flops to the ground, winces. Blood pours from his lip, gums. "Fine. We'll do it the hard way." Takes a GelOrange canister off his belt, pulls the pin, throw it toward Akari's window.

Jump, backflip, catch the canister in midair, pop the tip of my finger, engage the lockpick, jam it into the pinhole. Land and fire three shots at the Leader, one in the chest, one in the crotch, one in the face. PalCorp merc wriggles wildly, falls silent. Take the canister pin, still clutched in his hand, slip it back into place, hook the grenade to my jacket.

Akari emerges from the clinic with four crates of parts and equipment, stands in the doorway. "Was that as easy as it looked?"

Shake my head. "Almost let them blow you up." Green and white lights flicker in the distance, converging with the neon pinks and purples of the holos. PalCorp lights. More trouble coming this way. "We'd better go, now," I tell Akari.

She agrees. We run the crates to the Kento, lower the back seats, pop the hatchback and load them up. Climb into the car, boot it up, buckle in, and tear out of the parking lot. Push the Kento like I never have before, running it out on Undercity streets. The PerpetMot makes my mind clearer, my reflexes faster. Partying punks and druggies, toking vape, stroll or stumble into the street and we deftly slip around them. Haulers and Dencos and sanimechs chugging along, taking up the lane are no problem. Slide up onto the sidewalk, punch it, dart back in. Green and white lights can't keep up with us, might not even be trying, eventually fade away into the pollution and neon haze.

"Sorry about your shop," I say. "Probably won't be there if you come back."

"I won't be," Akari says. "But they'll enjoy the security drones."

Take us out of the Seventh, through the Fourth, and into the Second, where there's an easy exit to the outside. Along the way, see more action, corp troops trying to keep Undercity folks quiet, docile. Not working. Parties, real ragers with fireworks, kids whaling on holos, chronopanes, overwhelming corp troops, stripping them down, burning the unis. Newsfeed cams and reporters everywhere, capitalizing on the moment, making sure nothing goes unseen. News Haulers projecting holoscreens everywhere, every building and tower's showing the Commonwealth in rebirth. From the looks of it, it's not much different up top. Just better lit. Classy Overcity folks huddling around zecs and corp troops, keeping them contained. A blowout festival in the Wild Space between the Princess Towers. Hordes piling into the CommonCash headquarters in Eden. Massive protests, signs, chanting and marches filling Republic Park, spilling all over Ambrosia with crowds burning Cap and Bouquet merch, waving inverted Commonwealth flags. It's dawn.

Queue of vehicles at the gates in the Second, all honking, drivers yelling. Unbuckle and pop the gullwing. "Stay here," I tell Akari. Walk up the line, twenty cars deep, thirty. HomeCom's set up a blockade at the door. Eight guards, holding riot shields, pistols raised. Four drones hovering, flashing spotlights on everything. This won't do. Won't do at all. Activate the in-suit incog, turn on the reactive cloak, basically just disappear. Take out the drones first. Hunker behind a Hauler, poke my head out to fire four shock blasts, dead aim each time. Drones spark and sputter, wobble and crash to the ground. One of them lands right on a HomeCom guard. Makes seven left. Drivers start yelling and honking more. Few people climb out of the vehicles, watch me work, rather watch something work.

Sprint and the outermost guard, quick trip, one shot to stun, leave him on the ground. Leap over the next guard, power kick to the back, one more shock shot and he's down too. Five remaining guards start spinning around like lunatics. What professionalism from the corps. Rounds start flying everywhere. Cloak won't stop bullets. Get down and slide toward the next guard, rise up with an uppercut to jaw, grab his dead ass and throw him at the next one. Two more down, rumpled in a pile. Last three have heads on swivels, looking worried, can smell the sweat. Make short work of one, another shock shot drops him. Hop up onto the barricade, balance beam along and throw a roundhouse into the head of the next HomeCom merc, pop him once with the pistol for good measure. Last guard, shaking, drops his pistol and shield, starts yelling at the sky.

"Please don't hurt me! Please!"

Sidle up and whisper in his ear, the voice of an invisible predator, "Give you the count of five. One. Two. Three."

Sad HomeCom troop runs straight back into the Second. Doesn't look back.

Decloak and pull the barricades, hack the door control screen. Rush of warm wind pours in from the Wastes. Rush of harried drivers pours out. Sprint back to the Kento, strap in, and go. Activate the miniholo Jozy gave me, coordinates to the UC. No wandering or wondering necessary. Pull up to the compound's protective shielding in an hour. Akari gasps at what the Noncons built.

"I don't believe it," she says. "It's advanced."

"This, we're supposed to believe. Everything else, not so much."

Screen in the Kento starts chiming. Answer the ping. It's Jozy and Darius Spinks. "Run. Holy shit," Jozy says. "Are you alright? Did you... Did you cause what's happening in the Commonwealth?"

Nod. "Facilitated it. Can't take all the credit."

"It looks as though the people are taking back their city," Spinks says. "Let's hope that their intentions are good ones."

"Best we can do is hope," I say. "Teach a population to fish, so to speak. I've got one more with me." Point to Akari. "Can we come inside?"

Jozy beams. Shimmer-hair goes bright gold. "I've missed you."

"Mutual," I say. "I'm fond of you."

"The shield is lowering now," Spinks says. "Pull your vehicle into the garage behind Martin's. We'll help you unload."

^^^o

Spinks, Jozy, Martin help us get Akari's gear out of the back of the Kento. Martin sets Akari up with half his shop, in exchange for sharing some of her synth knowledge. Spinks gives us a tour of the UC, Akari gasping and overjoyed the entire time. Jozy and me peel off from the group when they enter the greenhouse, stroll back to her quarters, ours I suppose. It's a three room container home, little shielded courtyard in the center. Soon as we get inside, Jozy kisses me. Kiss her back. We undress, express the time and distance, now closed, between us two or three times. PerpetMot has distinct advantages. Jozy tells me so. Her shimmer-hair tells me more. Colors happen that defy nature, blues that turn fiery red and then bright yellow and purple all at once. We lay in bed together after, holding each other, talking about everything that went down in the Commonwealth, things we can do to improve the quarters, life in the UC, in the Wastes.

"I owe Akari a drink for making sure you didn't die in there," Jozy says as we redress.

"Same," I say. "Soon as she's done tinkering with Martin."

We go to the dining hall, meet up with Spinks, Akari, Martin, Dr. Olypha. Share a meal of fresh vegetables, rice noodles, straight from the greenhouse and paddies, drink red wine they fermented themselves. Martin keeps chattering about the newsfeed. Seems the folks of the Commonwealth had seized control of the Overcity. Number of zecs abandoned their positions, gave citizen access to the proprietary towers. Undercity remains a mess, chaos, looting, roving bands of troops causing trouble for anyone down enough to mess with easily. Spinks gives me assignments for the next day, maintenance, labor, that sort of thing. Don't mind a bit. Contributing in exchange for being part of the community's worth the effort. A day expanding the greenhouse, and helping with the harvest here. Another helping Martin reorg his shop there. Putting up a couple more structures one day. Letting Dr. Olypha, Akari, Martin and Jozy run some tests on my new synth body takes up a few days too. Month passes, entirely in bliss. Good work, good food, good love with Jozy. Sleep well, wake happy, day after day.

Newsfeeds share that the trouble's settled some in the Commonwealth. Government structures forming in the Undercity and the Overcity. Corps don't have a seat at the table. Former Caps and Bouqs expelled from service. The Under and the Over intend to come together, building a relationship, a pact, and a plan.

"The first ever Commonwealth United Governance Forum commences today, after weeks of distress and disarray have largely abated," the newsfeedcaster says. "Citizens representatives of the Undercity will meet with those of the Overcity to discuss paths forward for everyone in the Commonwealth. Each contingent is said to have plans, as yet undisclosed, to forge a new, inclusive, meaningful government. This story is developing and will be updated as soon as possible."◙

^^^o

Next morning, pack up the Kento. Upload all the cash I've got to the UC server. Not much, but enough to negotiate with the Commonwealth.

"Remind me why you're going back," Jozy says.

"Curious to see what's happening back there," I say. "Grab a few things from my old place, your old place, too."

"I don't know why you care, Run," she says. "Whatever happens, it'll be better than what it was. And that's thanks to you."

"She's right," Spinks interjects. "You altered the course of Commonwealth history. And by all accounts, for the better. I can understand your interest in surveying your handiwork. Just so long as you'll return to us."

Nod to the older man. "Won't be gone long. I like it here."

"Good man," Spinks says, slapping me on the shoulder. "We'll leave a light on for you."

"Thanks," I say. Turn to Jozy. "Five days, tops. I promise. Just something I have to see for myself. All those years of the newsfeed telling me one thing, of the corps telling me one thing, or the Caps and Bouqs. Tired of being told. Rather see it for myself."

She bites her lip. "You better stay out of trouble, and call me the moment that you get into some."

"Bet," I say. "Call you every night."

"You better." Her shimmer-hair goes fiery red.

Nod and smile. "Don't worry. Just going to check things out, see if I can help steer things in the right direction, and then I'm coming home."

Kiss her, long and hard. Shake Spinks' hand. Lift the gullwing of the Kento, climb in the driver's seat. "I'm fond of you, Jozy."

She replies in kind.

Close the gullwing, boot up the car, wave to my new family. Pull the Kento out of the UC protective shield into the Wastes. Start imagining how the Commonwealth might turn out, some kind of real, honest, honorable democracy. Stranger things have happened. Neighborhoods, buildings, streets are all the same. People've changed. They say, better the devil you know. The devil I know has a new face, and I want to see it up close.

Crank the Kento into high gear, hit the accelerator, and tear out across the Wastes. In the distance, the megacity glimmers like a jewel while a swirling, green and pink irradiated sandstorm churns just outside its walls.   /END▪

Acknowledgements

I started writing this book during the 2020 pandemic lockdown, so my deepest thanks goes to my wife, Jenny, for allowing me the space, and encouraging me to write while we were cooped up in a 580 sq. ft. apartment, for reading drafts of this, for always quietly fighting for Good in the world, and for loving me, always, superforevermuch. Love also goes to our dogs Toby (RIP) and Rocket, whose unconditional and unerring love kept us both going, and to Magnolia who just joined the family.

Huge thanks to my publishing partner, Shaunn, whose optimistic nihilism, wry wit, and belief in fighting for what's truly right and just has inspired aspects of this book. To Laura, who gave me her time to edit this book, and whose enthusiasm and positive feedback pushed me to get this manuscript off the screen and onto the printed page. And to writers Cory Doctorow, Kurt Vonnegut, Philip K. Dick, and William Gibson, Rod Serling, Ursula K. Le Guin, and countless films (*Blade Runner*, duh!) for laying the groundwork to talk about our problems through speculative stories.

About the Author

Nate Ragolia is a lifelong lover of science fiction and its power to imagine worlds more hopeful and inclusive than the real one. His first book, *There You Feel Free*, was published by 1888's Black Hill Press in 2015. Spaceboy Books reissued it in 2021. He's also the author of *The Retroactivist*, published by Spaceboy Books. He founded and edited *BONED*, a literary magazine, has created webcomics, currently hosts a podcast, and pets dogs.